Frederick Locker-Lampson

The Poems of Frederick Locker

Frederick Locker-Lampson

The Poems of Frederick Locker

ISBN/EAN: 9783337408022

Printed in Europe, USA, Canada, Australia, Japan

Cover: Foto ©Andreas Hilbeck / pixelio.de

More available books at **www.hansebooks.com**

THE POEMS

OF

FREDERICK LOCKER

AUTHORIZED EDITION

NEW YORK
FREDERICK A. STOKES & BROTHER
MDCCCLXXXIX

CONTENTS.

POEMS OF FREDERICK LOCKER.

THE OLD CRADLE.

AND this was your Cradle? Why,
    surely, my Jenny,
Such cosy dimensions go clearly to
    show
You were an exceedingly small picka-
    ninny
Some nineteen or twenty short sum-
    mers ago.

Your baby-days flow'd in a much-trou-
    bled channel;
I see you, as then, in your impotent
    strife,

A tight little bundle of wailing and flan-
    nel,
  Perplex'd with the newly-found fardel
    of Life.

To hint at an infantile frailty's a scan-
    dal ;
  Let bygones be bygones, for some-
    body knows
It was bliss such a Baby to dance and to
    dandle,—
  Your cheeks were so dimpled, so rosy
    your toes.

Ay, here is your Cradle ; and Hope, a
    bright spirit,
  With Love now is watching beside it,
    I know.
They guard the wee nest it was yours to
    inherit
  Some nineteen or twenty short sum-
    mers ago.

It is Hope gilds the future, Love wel-
    comes it smiling ;

Thus wags this old world, therefore
   stay not to ask,
" My future bids fair, is my future be-
   guiling ? "
If mask'd, still it pleases—then raise
   not its mask.

Is Life a poor coil some would gladly be
   doffing ?
He is riding post-haste who their
   wrongs will adjust ;
For at most 'tis a footstep from cradle
   to coffin—
From a spoonful of pap to a mouthful
   of dust.

Then smile as your future is smiling,
   my Jenny ;
I see you, except for those infantine
   woes,
Little changed since you were but a
   small pickaninny—
Your cheeks were so dimpled, so rosy
   your toes !

Ay, here is your Cradle, much, much
  to my liking,
  Though nineteen or twenty long winters have sped.
Hark! As I'm talking there's six o'clock
  striking,—
  It is time JENNY'S BABY should be in
  its bed.

1855.

PICCADILLY.

Minnie, in her hand a sixpence,
  Toddled off to buy some butter
(Minnie's pinafore was spotless)
  Back she brought it to the gutter ;
Gleeful, radiant, as she thus did,
Proud to be so largely trusted.

One, two, three small steps she'd taken
  Blissfully came little Minnie ;
When, poor bantling ! down she tumbled,
  Daubed her hands, and face, and pinny,
Dropping, too, the little slut, her
Pat of butter in the gutter.

Never creep back so despairing—
  Dry those eyes, my little fairy :
Most of us start off in high glee,
  Many come back "quite contrairy."
I've mourn'd sixpences in scores too,
Damaged hopes and pinafores too.
                    A SKETCH IN SEVEN DIALS.

PICCADILLY! Shops, palaces, bustle,
    and breeze,
The whirring of wheels, and the mur-
    mur of trees ;
By night or by day, whether noisy or
    stilly,
Whatever my mood is, I love Piccadilly.

Wet nights, when the gas on the pave-
    ment is streaming,
And young Love is watching, and old
    Love is dreaming,
And Beauty is whirling to conquest,
    where shrilly
Cremona makes nimble thy toes, Picca-
    dilly!

Bright days, when a stroll is my after-
    noon wont,
And I meet all the people I do know, or
    don't :—
Here is jolly old Brown, and his fair
    daughter Lillie—
No wonder some Pilgrims affect Picca-
    dilly!

See yonder pair riding, how fondly they
    saunter,
She smiles on her poet, whose heart's in
    a canter!
Some envy her spouse, and some covet
    her filly,
He envies them both,—he's an ass, Pic-
    cadilly!

Were I such a bride, with a slave at my
feet,
I would choose me a house in my fa-
vourite street;
Yes or no—I would carry my point,
willy-nilly :
If " no,"—pick a quarrel; if " yes,"—
Piccadilly!

From Primrose balcony, long ages
ago,
" Old Q." sat at gaze,—who now passes
below ?
A frolicsome statesman,—the Man of the
Day;
A laughing philosopher, gallant and
gay ;
Never darling of fortune more manfully
trod,
Full of years, full of fame, and the
world at his nod :
Can the thought reach his heart, and
then leave it more chilly—
" Old P. or Old Q.,—I must quit Picca-
dilly " ?

Life is chequer'd; a patchwork of
    smiles and of frowns;
We value its ups, let us muse on its
    downs;
There's a side that is bright, it will then
    turn us t'other,
One turn, if a good one, deserves yet
    another.
These downs are delightful, *these* ups
    are not hilly,—
Let us turn one more turn ere we quit
    Piccadilly.

1856.

THE OLD GOVERNMENT CLERK.

(OLD STYLE.)

A kindly, good man, quite a stranger to fame,
  His heart still is green, tho' his head shows a
    hoar lock;
Perhaps his particular star is to blame,—
  It may be he never took Time by the forelock.

WE knew an old scribe, it was "once
  on a time,"
An era to set sober datists despairing :
Then let them despair! Darby sat in a
  chair,
Near the Cross that gave name to the
  village of Charing.

Though silent and lean, Darby was not
  malign,
What hair he had left was more silver
  than sable ;

He had also contracted a curve in the
    spine,
From bending too constantly over a
    table.

His pay and expenditure, quite in ac-
    cord,
Were both on the strictest economy
    founded ;
His rulers were known as the Sealing-
    wax Board,
—They ruled where red tape and
    snug places abounded.

In his heart he look'd down on this dig-
    nified knot ;
And why? The forefather of one of
    these senators—
A rascal concern'd in the Gunpowder
    Plot—
Had been barber-surgeon to Darby's
    progenitors.

Poor fool, is not life a vagary of
    luck ?

For thirty long years—of genteel des-
    titution—
He'd been writing despatches; which
    means he had stuck
Some heads and some tails to much
    circumlocution.

This would seem rather weary and
    dreary; but, no!
Though strictly inglorious, his days
    were quiescent.
His red-tape was tied in a true-lover's
    bow
Every night when returning to Rose-
    mary Crescent.

There Joan meets him smiling, the
    young ones are there;
His coming is bliss to the half-dozen
    wee things;
The dog and the cat have a greeting to
    spare,
And Phyllis, neat-handed, is laying
    the tea-things.

East wind, sob eerily! Sing, kettle,
   cheerily!
  Baby's abed, but its father will rock
    it ;—
His little ones boast their permission to
    toast
That cake the good fellow brings home
    in his pocket.

This greeting the silent old Clerk under-
    stands,
  Now his friends he can love, had he
    foes he could mock them ;
So met, so surrounded, his bosom ex-
    pands,—
  Some hearts have more need of such
    homes to unlock them.

And Darby at least is resign'd to his lot ;
  And Joan, rather proud of the sphere
    he's adorning,
Has well-nigh forgotten that Gunpow-
    der Plot,—
  And *he* won't recall it till ten the next
    morning.

A day must be near when, in pitiful
    case,
He will drop from his Branch, like a
    fruit more than mellow;
Is he yet to be found in his usual place?
    Or is he already forgotten? poor
    fellow!

If still at his duty he soon will arrive;
    He passes this turning because it is
    shorter;
He always is here as the clock's going
    five
    —Where is he? . . . Ah, it is
    chiming the quarter!

1856.

THE PILGRIMS OF PALL MALL.

Her eyes and her hair
Are superb;
She stands in despair
On the kerb.
Quick, stranger, advance
To her aid :—
She's across, with a glance
You're repaid.
She's fair, and you're tall,
fal-lal-la !—
What will come of it all?
Chi lo sa !
CUPID ON THE CROSSING.

My little friend, so small, so neat,
Whom years ago I used to meet
    In Pall Mall daily,
How cheerily you tript away
To work, it might have been to play,
    You tript so gaily.

And Time trips too! This moral means
You then were midway in the teens

That I was crowning;
We never spoke, but when I smiled
At morn or eve, I know, dear Child,
    You were not frowning.

Each morning that we met, I think
One sentiment us two did link,
    Not joy, nor sorrow;
And then at eve, experience-taught,
Our hearts were lighter for the thought,—
    We meet to-morrow !

And you were poor, so poor! and why?
How kind to come, it was for my
    Especial grace meant !
Had you a chamber near the stars,—
A bird,—some treasured plants in jars.
    About your casement ?

Often I wander up and down,
When morning bathes the silent town
    In dewy glory
Perhaps, unwitting, I have heard
Your thrilling-toned canary-bird
    From that third story.

I've seen some change since last we
    met—
A patient little seamstress yet,
    On small wage striving,
Have you a Lilliputian spouse?
And do you dwell in some doll's
    house ?---
    Is baby thriving ?

My heart grows chill! Can soul like
    thine,
Weary of this dear World of mine,
    Have loosed its fetter,
To find a world, whose promised bliss
Is better than the best of this ?—
    And is it better?

Sometimes to Pall Mall I repair,
And see the damsels passing there ;
    But if I try to . . .
To get one glance, they look dis-
    creet,
As though they'd some one else to
    meet :—
    As have not *I* too ?

Yet still I often think upon
Our many meetings, come and gone,
    July—December !
Now let us make a tryst, and when,
Dear little soul, we meet again,
In some serener sphere, why then
    Thy friend remember.

1856.

MANY YEARS AFTER.

I SAW some books exposed for sale—
Some dear, and some—drama and
      tale—
    As dear as any :
A few, perhaps more orthodox
Or torn, were tumbled in a box—
    " *All these a penny.*"

I open'd one at hazard, but
Its leaves tho' soil'd were still uncut ;
    And yet before
I'd read a page, I felt indeed
A wish to cut that leaf, and read
      Some pages more.

A poet sang of what befel
When, years before, he'd paced Pall
      Mall ;

While walking thus—
A boy—he'd met a maiden.   (Then
Fair women all were brave, and men
    Were virtuous !)

They oft had met, he wonder'd why ;
He praised her sprightly bearing.   (I
    Believe he meant it :)
No word had pass'd, but if he smiled
Her eyes had seem'd to say (poor
    child !)
    " *I don't resent it.*"

And then this poet mused and grieved,
And spoke some kindly words, relieved
    By kindlier jest :
Then he, with sad, prophetic glance,
Bethought him she, ere then, perchance,
    Had found her rest.

Then I was minded how my Joy
Sometimes had told me of a boy
    With curly head—
" You know," she'd laugh (she then
    was well !)

" I used to meet him in Pall Mall—
    Ere I was wed."
And then, in fun, she'd vow " Good
    lack,
I'll go there now, and fetch thee back
    At least a curl ! "
She once was here, now she is gone !—
And so, you see, my wife was yon
    Bright little girl.

I am not one for shedding tears—
That boy's now dead, or bow'd with
    years—
    But see—*sometimes*
He'd thought of Her !—that made me
    weep ;
That's why I bought and why I keep
    His book of rhymes.

TEMPORA MUTANTUR!

He dropt a tear on Susan's bier,
*   He seem'd a most despairing swain :*
But bluer sky brought newer tie,
*   And—would he wish her back again?*
The moments fly, and when we die,
*   Will Philly Thistletop complain?*
She'll cry and sigh, and—dry her eye,
*   And let herself be woo'd again.*
                          A KIND PROVIDENCE.

YES, here, once more a traveller,
    I find the Angel Inn,
Where landlord, maids, and serving-
        men
    Receive me with a grin :
Surely they can't remember Me,
    My hair is grey and scanter ;
I'm changed, so changed since I was
        here—
    O tempora mutantur !

The Angel's not much alter'd since
    The happy month of June,

That brought me here with Pamela
    To spend our honeymoon.
Ah me, I even recollect
    The shape of this decanter !—
We've since been both much put about—
    O tempora mutantur !

Ay, there's the clock, and looking-
        glass
    Reflecting me again ;
She vow'd her Love was very fair,
    I see I'm very plain.
And there's that daub of Prince Leeboo :
    'Twas Pamela's fond banter
To fancy it resembled *me*—
    O tempora mutantur !

The curtains have been dyed ; but there,
    Unbroken, is the same,
The very same crack'd pane of glass
    On which I scratch'd her name.
Yes, there's her tiny flourish still ;
    It used to so enchant her
To link two happy names in one—
    O tempora mutantur !

What brought this pilgrim here? and
   why
Was Pamela away?
It may be she had found her grave,
   Or he had found her gay.
The fairest fade, the best of men
   Have met with a supplanter ;
I wish that I could like this cry
   Of tempora mutantur!

1856.

CIRCUMSTANCE.

THE ORANGE.

"At Brighton, just a year ago,
As I was leaving maison MUTTON,
My scarf got caught, it vex'd me so,
On that tall Captain Rose's button.
I thought he'd think me too inane
And awkward that September sunny,
And now September's come again!
And now we're married!—ain't it funny?"

EXTRACT FROM MRS. ROSE'S DIARY.

IT ripen'd by the river banks,
   Where, mask and moonlight aid-
      ing,
Dons Blas and Juan play their pranks,
   Dark Donnas serenading.

By Moorish damsel it was pluck'd,
   Beneath the golden day there;
By swain 'twas then in London suck'd—
   Who flung the peel away there.

He could not know in Pimlico,
  As little she in Seville,
That *I* should reel upon that peel,
  And—wish them at the devil.

1856.

ARCADIA.

Yes, Fortune deserves to be chidden,
It is a coincidence queer—
Whenever one wants to be hidden
Some blockhead is sure to appear !

THE healthy-wealthy-wise affirm
That early birds obtain the worm,—
    (The worm rose early too !)
Who scorns his couch should glean by
    rights
A world of pleasant sounds and sights
    That vanish with the dew.

Bright Phosphor, from his watch re-
    leased,
Now fading from the purple east,
    As morning gets the stronger ;—
The comely cock that vainly strives
To crow from sleep his drowsy wives,
    Who would be dozing longer.

Uxorious Chanticleer—And hark
Upraise thine eyes, and find the lark,
    The matutine musician
Who heavenward soars on rapture's
    wings,
Sought, yet unseen—who mounts and
    sings
    In musical derision.

From sea-girt pile, where nobles dwell,
A daughter waves her sire *Farewell*
    Across the sunlit water :
All these were heard or seen by one
Who stole a march upon that sun
    And then upon that daughter.

This dainty maid, the country's pride,
A white lamb trotting at her side,
    Had tript it through the park ;
A fond and gentle foster-dam,
Maybe she slumber'd with her lamb,
    Thus rising with the lark.

The lambkin frisk'd, the lady fain
Would coax him back, she call'd in
    vain,

The rebel proved unruly ;
The sun came streaming o'er the lake ;—
One followed for the maid's dear sake,
A happy fellow truly.

The maid gave chase, the lambkin ran
As only woolly truant can
    Who never felt a crook ;
But stayed at length, as if disposed
To drink, where tawny sands disclosed
    The margin of a brook.

His mistress, who had followed fast,
Cried, " Little rogue, you're caught at
        last ;
    You've made me lose my shoe ! "
She then the wanderer convey'd
Where kindly shrubs, in branching
        shade,
    Were screen and shelter too :

And timidly she glanced around,
All fearful lest the slightest sound
    Might mortal footfall be ;
Then shrinkingly she stept aside

One moment—and her garter tied
    The truant to a tree.

Perhaps the world would like to know
The hue of this enchanting bow,
    And if 'twere silk or laced ;
No, not from him !   Be pleased to think
It might be either—blue or pink ;
    'Twas tied with maiden taste.

Suffice it that the child was fair
As Una, blythe, with golden hair,
    And come of high degree ;
And though her feet were pure from
      stain,
She turned her to the brook again,
    And laved them dreamingly.

Awhile she sat in maiden mood,
And watched the shadows from the
    wood,
    That varied on the stream ;
And as each pretty foot she dipp'd,
The little waves rose crystal-lipp'd
    In welcome, as 'twould seem.

Yet reveries are fleeting things,
That come and go on whimsy wings ;
    As kindly fancy taught her,
The Fair her tender day-dream nursed ;
But when the light-blown bubble burst,
    She wearied of the water ;

Betook her to the spot where, yet,
Safe tether'd lay her captured pet,
    To roving tastes a martyr ;
But all at once she spied a change,
And   scream'd (it seem'd so very
    strange !)—
    Cried Echo, *Where's my garter ?* . .

The Lady led her lambkin home !
Maybe she thought, "No more we'll
    roam
    At peep of day together ; "
Well, if they do, or if they don't,
It's pretty clear that roam she won't
    Without an extra tether.

A pure white stone will mark this
    morn ;

He wears a prize, one gladly worn,
    Love's gage, though not intended ;
And let him wear it near his heart,
Till sun, and moon, and stars depart,
    And chivalry has ended.

Dull World !   He now resigns to you
The tinsel star, and ribbon blue,
    That pride for folly barters :
He'll bear his cross amid your jars,
His ribbon prize, and thank his stars
    He does not crave your garters.

1849.

THE CASTLE IN THE AIR.

The old, old tale ! ay, there's the smart :
Her heart, or what she call'd her heart,
Was hard as granite :
Who breaks a heart and then omits
To gather up the broken bits,
Is heartless, Janet.

YOU shake your saucy curls, and vow
I build no airy castles now ;
You smile, and you are thinking too,
He's nothing else on earth to do.

It needs romance, my Lady Fair,
To build a Castle in the Air :
Ethereal brick, and rainbow beam,
The gossamer of fancy's dream ;
Much, too, the architect may lack,
Who labours in the Zodiac,
To rear what I, from chime to chime,
Attempted once upon a time.

My Castle was a gay retreat
  In Air, that rather gusty shire,
A cherub's model country seat,—
  Could model cherub such require.
Nor twinge nor tax existence tortured,
Even the cherub spared my orchard !
No worm destroyed the gourd I planted,
And showers came when rain was wanted.
I own'd a tract of purple mountain,
A sweet mysterious haunted fountain,
A terraced lawn, a summer lake,
  By sun- or moon-beam always burn-
    ish'd ;
And then my cot, by some mistake,
  Unlike most cots, was neatly fur-
    nish'd.—
A trellis'd porch, a pictured hall,
A Hebe laughing from the wall ;
  Vases, Etruscan and Cathay ;
While under arms and armour wreath'd
In trophied guise, the marble breathed—
  A peering faun—a startled fay.

On silken cushion, laced and pearl'd,
A shaggy pet from Skye was curl'd ;

While, drowsy-eyed, would dosing swing
A parrot in his golden ring.

All this I saw one happy day,
  And more than now I care to name ;
Here, lately shut, that work-box lay,
    There stood your own embroidery
      frame.
And over this piano bent
A Form from some pure region lent.
Her auburn tresses darkly shone
In clusters, lovely as your own ;
And as her fingers touch'd the keys,
How strangely they resembled these !

Yes, you, you only, Lady Fair,
Adorn'd a Castle in the Air,
Where Life, without the least foundation
Became a charming occupation.
We heard with much sublime disdain
The far-off thunder of Cockaigne ;
And saw through rifts of silver cloud
The rolling smoke that hid the crowd.
With souls released from earthly tether
We hymn'd the tender moon together.

Our sympathy from night to noon
Rose crescent with that crescent moon ;
The night was briefer than the song,
And happy as the day was long.
We lived and loved in cloudless climes,
And died (in verse) a thousand times !

Yes, you, you only, Lady Fair,
Adorn'd my Castle in the Air.
Now, tell me, could you dwell content
In such a baseless tenement ?
Say, could so delicate a flower
Exist in such a breezy bower ?
Because, if you would settle in it,
'Twere built for love in half a minute.

What's love ?   Why love (for two) at
        best
Is only a delightful jest ;
But not so nice for one or three,—
I only wish you'd jest with me.

You shake your head and wonder why
    A denizen of dear Mayfair
Should be so silly as to try

And build a Castle in the Air.
" I've music, books, and all," you say,
" To make the gravest lady gay.
I'm told my essays mark research,
My sketches have endow'd a church ;
I've partners who have brilliant parts—
I've lovers who have broken hearts.
Poor Polly would not care to fly,
And Mop, you know, was born in Skye.
To realise your *tête-à-tête*
Might jeopardise a giddy pate ;
Indeed, my much devoted vassal,
I'm sorry that you've built your Castle ! "

The lady's smile showed no remorse,—
  " My worthless toy has lost its gild-
    ing,"
I murmur'd with pathetic force,
  " And here's an end of castle-build-
    ing ; "
Then strode away in mood morose
To blame the Sage of Careless Close ;
He trifled with my tale of sorrow,—
" What's marr'd to-day is made to-
  morrow ;

Romance can roam not far from home,
  Knock gently, she must answer soon;
I'm sixty-five, and yet I strive
  To hang my garland on the moon."

1848.

A WISH.

To the south of the church, and beneath
    yonder yew,
A pair of child lovers I've seen ;
More than once were they there, and
    the years of the two
When united, might number thirteen.

They sat by a grave that had never a
    stone
The name of the dead to determine ;
It was Life paying Death a brief visit,
    —a known
And a notable text for a sermon.

They tenderly prattled; oh what did
    they say ?
The turf on that hillock was new.
Little Friends, could ye know aught of
    death or decay ?
Could the dead be regardful of you ?

I wish to believe, and believe it I
    must,
That there her loved father was laid :
I wish to believe—I will take it on
    trust—
That father knew all that they said.

My Own, you are five, very nearly the
    age
Of that poor little fatherless child,
And some day a true-love your heart
    will engage,
When on earth I my last may have
    smiled.

Then come to my grave, like a good lit-
    tle lass,
Where'er it may happen to be ;
And if any daisies should peer through
    the grass,
Be sure they are kisses from me.

And place not a stone to distinguish my
    name,
For stranger and gossip to see ;

But come with your lover, as these lov-
    ers came,
And talk to him sweetly of me.

And while you are smiling, your father
    will smile
Such a dear little daughter to have ;
But mind,—oh yes, mind you are happy
    the while—
I wish you to visit my grave.

1856.

GERALDINE GREEN.

I.

THE SERENADE.

If pathos should thy bosom stir
To tears more sweet than laughter,
Then bless its kind interpreter,
And love him ever after !

LIGHT slumber is quitting
  The eyelids it prest ;
The fairies are flitting,
  Who charm'd thee to rest.
Where night dews were falling,
  Now feeds the wild bee ;
The starling is calling,
  My darling, for thee.

The wavelets are crisper
  That thrill the shy fern ;
The leaves fondly whisper,
  " We wait thy return."

Arise then, and hazy
    Distrust from thee fling,
For sorrows that crazy
    To-morrows may bring.

A vague yearning smote us,
    But wake not to weep ;
My bark, Love, shall float us
    Across the still deep,
To isles where the lotus
    Erst lulled thee to sleep.
1861.

II.

MY LIFE IS A ———.

Fair Emma mocks my trials,
She pokes her jokes in Sevenoaks
At me in Seven Dials.—

AT Worthing, an exile from Geraldine
    G——,
How aimless, how wretched an exile is
    he !
Promenades are not even prunella and
    leather
To lovers, if lovers can't foot them
    together.

He flies the parade, by the ocean he
    stands ;
He traces a " Geraldine G." on the
    sands ;
Only " G.!" though her loved patro-
    nymic is " Green,"—
" I will not betray thee, my own Geral-
    dine."

The fortunes of men have a time and a
    tide,
And Fate, the old Fury, will not be
    denied ;
That name was, of course, soon wiped
    out by the sea,—
She jilted the exile, did Geraldine G.

They meet, but they never have spoken
    since that ;
He hopes she is happy—he knows she
    is fat ;
She, wooed on the shore, now is wed in
    the Strand,—
And *I*—it was I wrote her name on the
    sand.
    1854.

VANITY FAIR.

" VANITAS vanitatum " has rung in the
    ears
Of gentle and simple for thousands of
    years ;
The wail still is heard, yet its notes never
    scare
Either simple or gentle from Vanity
    Fair.

I often hear people abusing it, yet
There the young go to learn and the old
    to forget ;
The mirth may be feigning, the sheen
    may be glare,
But the gingerbread's gilded in Vanity
    Fair.

Old Dives there rolls in his chariot, but
    mind

Atra Cura is up with the lackeys be-
  hind ;
Joan trudges with Jack,—are the Sweet-
  hearts aware
Of the trouble that waits them in Vanity
  Fair ?

We saw them all go, and we something
  may learn
Of the harvest they reap when we see
  them return.
The tree was enticing, its branches are
  bare,—
Heigho for the promise of Vanity Fair.

That stupid old Dives, once honest
  enough,
His honesty sold for star, ribbon, and
  stuff ;
And Joan's pretty face has been clouded
  with care
Since Jack bought her ribbons at Vanity
  Fair.

Contemptible Dives! too credulous
  Joan !

Yet we all have a Vanity Fair of our
    own ;
My son, you have yours, but you need
    not despair—
I own I've a weakness for Vanity Fair.

Philosophy halts—wise counsels are
    vain,
We go, we repent, we return there
    again ;
To-night you will certainly meet with us
    there—
So come and be merry in Vanity Fair.

   1852.

BRAMBLE-RISE.

These days were soon the days of yore ;
Six summers pass, and then
That musing man would see once more
The fountain in the glen.
                              THE RUSSET PITCHER.

WHAT changes meet my wistful eyes
In quiet little Bramble-Rise,
    The pride of all the shire ;
How altered is each pleasant nook ;—
And used the dumpy church to look
    So dumpy in the spire ?

This village is no longer mine ;
And though the Inn has changed its
      sign,
    The beer may not be stronger ;
The river, dwindled by degrees,
Is now a brook, the cottages
    Are cottages no longer.

The mud is brick, the thatch is slate,
The pound has tumbled out of date,
    And all the trees are stunted :
Surely these thistles once grew figs,
These geese were swans, and once these
    pigs
    More musically grunted.

Where boys and girls pursued their
    sports
A locomotive puffs and snorts,
    And gets my malediction ;
The turf is dust—the elves are fled—
The ponds have shrunk—and tastes have
    spread
To photograph and fiction.

Ah, there's a face I know again,
There's Patty trotting down the lane
    To fill her pail with water ;
Yes, Patty ! but I fear she's not
The tricksy Pat that used to trot,
    But Patty,—Patty's daughter !

And has she, too, outlived the spells
Of breezy hills and silent dells

Where childhood loved to ramble?
Then life was thornless to our ken,
And, Bramble-Rise, thy hills were then
    A rise without a bramble.

Whence comes the change? 'Twere
    simply told;
For some grow wise, and some grow
    cold,
    And all feel time and trouble:
If life an empty bubble be,
How sad for those who cannot see
    The rainbow in the bubble!

And senseless too, for Madame Fate
Is not the fickle reprobate
    That moody sages thought her;
My heart leaps up, and I rejoice,
As falls upon my ear thy voice,
    My little friskful daughter.

Come hither, fairy, perch on these
Thy most unworthy father's knees,
    And tell him all about it.
Are dolls a sham? Can men be base?

When gazing on thy blessed face
    I'm quite prepared to doubt it.

Though life is call'd a doleful jaunt,
Though earthly joys, the wisest grant,
    Have no enduring basis ;
It's pleasant in this lower sphere,
To find with Puss, my daughter dear,
    A little cool oasis !

Oh, may'st thou some day own, sweet
    elf,
A pet just like thy winsome self,
    Her sanguine thoughts to borrow ;
Content to use her brighter eyes,
Accept her childish ecstasies,—
    If need be, share her sorrow.

The wisdom of thy prattle cheers
This heart ; and when, outworn in years,
    And homeward I am starting,
Lead me, my darling, gently down
To life's dim strand : the skies may
    frown,—
    But weep not for our parting.
April, 1857.

OLD LETTERS.

Have sorrows come? Has pleasure sped?
Is earthly bliss an empty bubble?
Is some one dull, or something dead?
O may I, mayn't I share your trouble?
　　　*　　　　　*
Ay, so it is, and is it fair?
Poor men (your elders and your betters!)
Who can't look pretty in despair,
Feel quite as sad about their letters.
HER LETTERS.

OLD letters! wipe away the tear
　For lines so pale, so vainly worded;
A Pilgrim finds his journey here
　Since first his youthful loins were
　　girded.

Yes, here are wails from Clapham
　　Grove;
　How could philosophy expect us
To live with Dr. Wise, and love
　Rice pudding and the Greek De-
　　lectus?

How strange to commune with the
    Dead !
Dead joys, dead loves ; and wishes
    thwarted :
Here's cruel proof of friendships fled,
    And, sad enough, of friends departed.

Yes, here's the offer that I wrote
    In '33 to Lucy Diver ;
And here John Wylie's begging note,—
    He never paid me back a stiver.

Here's news from Paternoster Row ;
    How mad I was when first I learnt it !
They would not take my Book, and now
    I wish to goodness I had burnt it.

A ghastly bill ! " *I disapprove.*"
    And yet She help'd me to defray it :—
What tokens of a mother's love !
    O bitter thought,—I can't repay it.

And here's a score of notes at last,
    With " *Love*" and " *Dove*," and
    " *Sever, Never*";

Though hope, though passion may be
    past,
Their perfume seems—ah, sweet as
    ever.

A human heart should beat for two,
    Whate'er may say your single scorn·
       ers ;
And all the hearths I ever knew
    Had got a pair of chimney-corners.

See here a double violet—
Two locks of hair—A deal of scandal ;
I'll burn what only brings regret—
    Kitty, go, fetch a lighted candle.

  1856.

MY FIRST-BORN.

Of a worthless old Block she's the dearest of Chips,
For what nonsense she talks when she opens her
lips.

LITTLE PITCHER.

"HE shan't be their namesake, the
    rather
  That both are such opulent men :
His name shall be that of his father,
  My Benjamin, shorten'd to *Ben.*

"Yes, *Ben,* though it cost him a portion
  In each of my relatives' wills :
I scorn such baptismal extortion—
  (That creaking of boots must be
    Squills.)

"It is clear, though his means may be
    narrow,
  This infant his Age will adorn ;
I shall send him to Oxford from Har-
    row,—
  I wonder how soon he'll be born !"

A spouse thus was airing his fancies
  Below, 'twas a labour of love,
And was calmly reflecting on Nancy's
  More practical labour above ;

Yet while it so pleased him to ponder,
  Elated, at ease, and alone ;
That pale, patient victim up yonder
  Had budding delights of her own :

Sweet thoughts, in their essence diviner
  Than paltry ambition and pelf;
A cherub, no babe will be finer !
  Invented and nursed by herself;

At breakfast, and dining, and tea-ing,
  An appetite naught can appease,
And quite a Young-Reasoning-Being
  When call'd on to yawn and to sneeze.

What cares that heart, trusting and
      tender,
  For fame or avuncular wills ?
Except for the name and the gender,
  She's almost as tranquil as Squills.

That father, in reverie centred,
  Dumbfounder'd, his thoughts in a
    whirl,
Heard Squills, as the creaking boots
    enter'd,
  Announce that his Boy was—a Girl.

THE WIDOW'S MITE.

A WIDOW—she had only one!
A puny and decrepit son;
    But, day and night,
Though fretful oft, and weak and small,
A loving child, he was her all—
    The Widow's Mite.

The Widow's Mite—ay, so sustain'd,
She battled onward, nor complain'd
    Tho' friends were fewer :
And while she toil'd for daily fare,
A little crutch upon the stair
    Was music to her.

I saw her then—and now I see
That, though resign'd and cheerful, she
    Has sorrow'd much :
She has, HE gave it tenderly,
Much faith ; and, carefully laid by,
    A little crutch.

1856.

ST. GEORGE'S, HANOVER SQUARE.

Why little Di should throw me over
I never knew,—I can't discover,
*   Or even guess;*
Maybe Smith's lyrics she decided
Were sweeter than the sweetest I did,—
*   I acquiesce.*

SHE pass'd up the aisle on the arm of
    her sire,
A delicate lady in bridal attire,
    Fair emblem of virgin simplicity;
Half London was there, and, my word,
    there were few
That stood by the altar, or hid in a pew,
    But envied Lord Nigel's felicity.

Beautiful Bride!—So meek in thy splen-
    dour,
So frank in thy love, and its trusting
    surrender,
    Departing you leave us the town
    dim!

May happiness wing to thy bower, un-
    sought,
And may Nigel, esteeming his bliss as
    he ought,
    Prove worthy thy worship,—con-
      found him !

A HUMAN SKULL.

A HUMAN Skull! I bought it passing
    cheap,
    Indeed 'twas dearer to its first em-
      ployer!
I thought mortality did well to keep
    Some mute memento of the Old De-
      stroyer.

Time was, some may have prized its
    blooming skin ;
    Here lips were woo'd, perhaps, in
      transport tender ;
Some may have chuck'd what was a
    dimpled chin,
    And never had my doubt about its
      gender.

Did she live yesterday or ages back?
    What colour were the eyes when
      bright and waking?

And were your ringlets fair, or brown,
    or black,
  Poor little head ! that long has done
    with aching ?

It may have held (to shoot some random
    shots)
  Thy brains, Eliza Fry! or Baron
    Byron's ;
The wits of Nelly Gwynn, or Doctor
    Watts—
  Two quoted bards. Two philanthropic
    sirens.

But this I trust is clearly understood ;
  If man or woman, if adored or hated—
Whoever own'd this Skull was not so
    good,
  Nor quite so bad as many may have
    stated.

Who love can need no special type of
    Death ;
  Death steals his icy hand where Love
    reposes ;

Alas for love, alas for fleeting breath—
  Immortelles bloom with Beauty's bridal
    roses.

O true-love mine, what lines of care are
    these?
  The heart still lingers with its golden
    hours,
But fading tints are on the chestnut-
    trees,
  And where is all that lavish wealth
    of flowers?

The end is near. Life lacks what once
    it gave,
Yet death has promises that call for
    praises ;
A very worthless rogue may dig the
    grave,
  But hands unseen will dress the turf
    with daisies.

1860.

TO MY OLD FRIEND POSTUMUS.

(J. G.)

And, like yon clocke, when twelve shalle sound
To call our soules away,
Together may our hands be found,
An earnest that we praie.

My Friend, our few remaining years
  Are hastening to an end,
They glide away, and lines are here
  That time can never mend;
Thy blameless life avails thee not,—
  My Friend, my dear old Friend!

Death lifts a burthen from the poor,
  And brings the weary rest,
But oft from earth's green orchard trees
  The canker takes our best—
The Well-beloved! she bloom'd, and
    now
  The turf is on her breast.

Alas for love ! This peaceful home !
  The darling at my knee !
My own dear wife ! Thyself, old Friend !
  And must it come to me,
That any face shall fill my place
  Unknown to them and thee ?

Ay, all too vainly are we screen'd
  From peril, day and night ;
Those awful rapids must be shot,
  Our shallop will be slight ;—
O pray that then we may descry
  Some cheering beacon-light.

LOULOU AND HER CAT.

I'm nervous too, I hate a cat!
Extremely so; but, as for that,
It is not only cat or rat,
Or haunted room, or ghostly chat,
That makes my heart go pit-a-pat.

GOOD pastry is vended
  In Cité Fadette ;
Maison Pons can make splendid
  Brioche and *galette.*

M'sieu Pons is so fat that
  He's laid on the shelf ;
Madame had a cat that
  Was fat as herself.

Long hair, soft as satin,
  A musical purr,
'Gainst the window she'd flatten
  Her delicate fur.

I drove Lou to see what
  These worthies were at,—
In rapture, cried she, " What
  An exquisite cat !

" What whiskers !   She's purring
  All over.   Regale
Our eyes, *Puss*, by stirring
  Your feathery tail !

" *M'sieu Pons*, will you sell her ? "
  " *Ma femme est sortie*,
Your offer I'll tell her ;
  But—will she ? " says he.

Yet *Pons* was persuaded
  To part with the prize :
(Our bargain was aided,
  My Lou, by your eyes !)

From his *legitime* save him,—
  My spouse I prefer,—
For I warrant *his* gave him
  Un mauvais quart d'heure.

I'm giving a pleasant
   Grimalkin to Lou,—
Ah, *Puss*, what a present
   I'm giving to you!

THE NYMPH OF THE WELL.

Whoever shall win you,—a Fan or a Phœbe,
Of course of all beauty she must be the belle ;
If at Tunbridge you chance to fall in with a Hebe,
You will not fall out with a draught from the
Well !

SHE smiled as she gave him a draught
    from the springlet,—
O Tunbridge, thy waters are bitter,
    alas !
But love has an ambush in dimple and
    ringlet ;
   " Thy health, pretty maiden ! " He
    emptied the glass.

He saw, and he loved her, nor cared
    he to quit her ;
   The oftener he came there, the
    longer he stay'd ;
Indeed though the spring was exceed-
    ingly bitter,
We found him eternally pledging the
    maid.

A *preux chevalier*, and but lately a
 cripple,
He met with his hurt where a regi-
 ment fell ;
But worse was he wounded when stay-
 ing to tipple
A bumper to " Phœbe, the Nymph
 of the Well."

Some swore he was old, that his laurels
 were faded,
All vow'd she was vastly too nice for
 a nurse ;
But love never looks on the matter as
 they did,—
She took the brave soldier for better
 or worse.

And here is the home of her fondest
 election,
The walls may be worn, but the ivy is
 green ;
And here she has tenderly twined her
 affection
Around a true soldier who bled for
 the Queen.

See, yonder he sits, where the church-
    bells invite us,
  What child is that spelling the epi-
    taphs there ?
'Tis the joy of his age ; and may love
    so requite us,
  When time shall have broken, or
    sickness, or care.

And when he is gone, thro' her widow-
    hood lowly
  He'll still live as Chivalry's Light to
    her son :
But only on days that are high and are
    holy
  She will show him the Cross that her
    hero had won.

So taught, he will rather take after his
    father,
  And wear a long sword to our ene-
    mies' loss ;
And some day or other he'll bring to
    his mother
  Victoria's gift—the Victoria Cross !

And then will her darling, like all good
    and true ones,
Console and sustain her—the weak
    and the strong—
And some day or other two black eyes
    or blue ones
Will smile on his path as he jour-
    neys along.

HER QUIET RESTING-PLACE.

At Susan's name the fancy plays
With chiming thoughts of early days,
And hearts unwrung :
When all too fair our future smiled,
When she was Mirth's adopted child,
And I was young.

*   *   *   *

And summer smiles, but summer spells
Can never charm where sorrow dwells—
No maiden fair,
Or sad, or gay, the passer sees,—
And still the much-loved elder trees
Throw shadows there.

HER quiet resting-place is far away ;
   None dwelling there can tell you her
      sad story.
The stones are mute.   The stones could
      only say,
" *A humble spirit pass'd away to*
      glory."

She loved the murmur of this mighty
      town ;

The lark rejoiced her from its lattice
　　prison ;
A streamlet lulls her now, the bird has
　　flown,
　　Some dust is waiting there—a soul has
　　risen.

No city smoke to stain the heather
　　bells ;
　　Sigh, gentle winds, around my lone
　　love sleeping ;—
She bore her burthen here, but now she
　　dwells
　　Where scorner never came, and none
　　are weeping.

My name was falter'd with her parting
　　breath ;
　　These arms were round my darling at
　　the latest ;
All scenes of death are woe, but painful
　　death
　　In those we dearly love is woe the
　　greatest.

I could not die : HE willed it otherwise ;
 My lot is here, and sorrow, wearing
  older,
Weighs down the heart, but does not
  fill the eyes,—
 Even my friends may think that I am
  colder.

But when at times I steal away from
  these,
 To find her grave, and pray to be forgiven,
And when I watch beside her on my
  knees,
 I think I am a little nearer heaven.

1861.

REPLY TO A LETTER ENCLOSING
A LOCK OF HAIR.

She laugh'd—she climb'd the giddy height ;—
I held that climber small ;
I even held her rather tight,
For fear that she should fall.
A dozen girls were chirping round,
Like five-and-twenty linnets ;—
I must have held her, I'll be bound,
Some five-and-twenty minutes.

YES, you were false, and, if I'm free,
   I still would be the slave of yore ;
Then, join'd, our years were thirty-three,
   And now,—yes, now I'm thirty-four.
And though you were not learnèd—well,
   I was not anxious you should grow
     so ;—
I trembled once beneath her spell
   Whose spelling was extremely so-so.

Bright season ! why will Memory
   Still haunt the path our rambles
     took,—

The sparrow's nest that made you cry,
  The lilies captured in the brook ?
I'd lifted you from side to side,
  (You seem'd as light as that poor
    sparrow ;)
I know who wish'd it twice as wide,
  I think *you* thought it rather narrow.

Time was, indeed a little while,
  My pony could your heart compel ;
And once, beside the meadow-stile,
  I thought you loved me just as well ;
I'd kiss'd your cheek ; in sweet surprise
  Your troubled gaze said plainly,
    " Should he ? "
But doubt soon fled those daisy eyes,—
  " He could not mean to vex me, could
    he ? "

The brightest eyes are soonest sad,
  But your rose cheek, so lightly sway'd,
Could ripple into dimples glad ;
  For oh, fair friend, what mirth we
    made !
The brightest tears are soonest dried,

But your young love and dole were
    stable ;
You wept when dear old Rover died,
    You wept—and dress'd your dolls in
    sable.

As year succeeds to year, the more
    Imperfect life's fruition seems ;
Our dreams, as baseless as of yore,
    Are not the same enchanting dreams.
The girls I love now vote me slow—
    How dull the boys who once seem'd
    witty !
Perhaps I'm growing old, I know
    I'm still romantic, more's the pity.

Vain the regret—to few, perchance,
    Unknown, and profitless to all :
The wisely-gay, as years advance,
    Are gaily-wise.   Whate'er befall,
We'll laugh at folly, whether seen
    Under a chimney or a steeple ;
At   yours,   at   mine — our   own,   I
    mean,
    As well as that of other people.

I'm fond of fun, the mental dew
  Where wit, and truth, and ruth are
    blent;
And yet I've known a prig or two,
  Who, wanting all, were all content!
To say I hate such dismal men
  Might be esteem'd a strong assertion;
If I've blue devils, now and then,
  I make them dance for my diversion.

And here's your letter debonair—
  "*My friend, my dear old friend of
    yore,*"
And is this curl your daughter's hair?
  I've seen the Titian tint before.
Are we the pair that used to pass
  Long days beneath the chestnut
    shady?
Then you were such a pretty lass—
  I'm told you're now as fair a lady.

I've laugh'd to hide the tear I shed,
  As when the Jester's bosom swells,
And mournfully he shakes his head,
  We hear the jingle of his bells.

A jesting vein your poet vex'd,
  And this poor rhyme, the Fates de-
    termine,
Without a parson or a text,
  Has proved a rather prosy sermon.

  1859.

THE BEAR PIT.

IN THE ZOOLOGICAL GARDENS.

It seems that poor Bruin has never had peace
'Twixt bald men in Bethel, and wise men in grease.
                                        OLD ADAGE.

WE liked the bear's serio-comical face,
As he loll'd with a lazy, a lumbering
    grace ;
Said Slyboots to me (just as if *she* had
    none),
" Papa, let's give Bruin a bit of your
    bun."

Says I, " A plum bun might please wist-
    ful old Bruin,
He can't eat the stone that the cruel
    boy threw in ;
Stick *yours* on the point of mamma's
    parasol,
And then he will climb to the top of the
    pole.

"Some bears have got two legs, and
    some have got more,
Be good to old bears if they've no legs
    or four ;
Of duty to age you should never be
    careless,—
My dear, I am bald, and I soon may be
    hairless !

"The gravest aversion exists among
    bears
From rude forward persons who give
    themselves airs,—
We know how some graceless young
    people were maul'd
For plaguing a Prophet, and calling him
    bald.

"Strange ursine devotion ! Their dan-
    cing-days ended,
Bears die to 'remove' what, in life,
    they defended :
They succour'd the Prophet, and, since
    that affair,
The bald have a painful regard for the
    bear."

MY MORAL—Small people may read it,
    and run.
(The child has my moral,—the bear has
    my bun.)

MY NEIGHBOUR ROSE.

And knavves and wenches, less adoe,
  My neighbour is astir :
By cockke *and* pie *she lutes it too*
  Behynde the silver fir !

THOUGH walls but thin our hearths
    divide,
We're strangers, dwelling side by side ;
How gaily all your days must glide
    Unvex'd by labour.
I've seen you weep, and could have
    wept ;
I've heard you sing, (and might have
    slept !)
Sometimes I hear your chimney swept,
    My charming neighbour !

Your pets are mine. Pray what may
    ail
The pup, once eloquent of tail ?
I wonder why your nightingale

Is mute at sunset.
Your puss, demure and pensive, seems
Too fat to mouse. Much she esteems
Yon sunny wall, and, dozing, dreams
    Of mice she once ate.

Our tastes agree. I dote upon
Frail jars, turquoise and celadon,
The *Wedding March* of Mendelssohn,
    And *Penseroso*.
When sorely tempted to purloin
Your *pietà* of Marc Antoine,
Fair virtue doth fair play enjoin,
    Fair Virtuoso!

At times an Ariel, cruel-kind,
Will kiss my lips, and stir your blind,
And whisper low, " She hides behind ;
    Thou art not lonely."
The tricksy sprite would erst assist
At hush'd Verona's moonlight tryst ;—
Sweet Capulet, thou wert not kiss'd
    By light winds only.

I miss the simple days of yore,
When two long braids of hair you wore,

And *chat botté* was wonder'd o'er,
   In corner cosy.
But gaze not back for tales like those :
It's all in order, I suppose ;
The Bud is now a blooming ROSE,—
   A rosy-posy !

Indeed, farewell to bygone years ;
How wonderful the change appears ;
For curates now, and cavaliers,
   In turn perplex you :
The last are birds of feather gay,
Who swear the first are birds of prey ;
I'd scare them all had I my way,
   But that might vex you.

Sometimes I've envied, it is true,
That hero, joyous twenty-two,
Who sent *bouquets* and *billets doux*,
   And wore a sabre.
The rogue ! how close his arm he
   wound
About her waist, who never frown'd.
He loves you, Child.   Now, is he bound
   To love *my* neighbour ?

The bells are ringing. As is meet
White favours fascinate the street,
Sweet faces greet me, rueful-sweet
    'Twixt tears and laughter :
They crowd the door to see her go,
The bliss of one brings many woe ;
Oh, kiss the bride, and I will throw
    The old shoe after.

What change in one short afternoon,
My own dear neighbour gone,—so soon !
Is yon pale orb her honey-moon
    Slow rising hither ?
O Lady, wan and marvellous !
How oft have we held commune thus ;
Sweet memory shall dwell with us,—
    And joy go with her.

1861.

THE OLD OAK-TREE AT HAT-
FIELD BROADOAK.

What? Tell you that tale? Come, a tale with a
sting
Would be rather too much of an excellent thing!
I can't point a moral, or sing you the song,
My Years are too short—and your Ears are too
long.
LITTLE PITCHER.

A MIGHTY growth !   The county side
Lamented when the Giant died,
    For England loves her trees :
What misty legends round him cling ;
How lavishly he once could fling
    His acorns to the breeze !

Who struck a thousand roots in fame,
Who gave the district half its name,
    Will not be soon forgotten :
Last spring he show'd but one green
     bough,
The red leaves hang there yet,—and
     now
His very props are rotten !

Elate, the thunderbolt he braved,
For centuries his branches waved
    A welcome to the blast ;
From reign to reign he bore a spell ;
No forester had dared to fell
    What time has fell'd at last.

The Monarch wore a leafy crown,—
And wolves, ere wolves were hunted
    down,
    Found shelter in his gloom ;
Unnumber'd squirrels frolick'd free,
Glad music fill'd the gallant Tree
    From stem to topmost bloom.

It's hard to say, 'twere vain to seek,
When first he ventured forth, a meek
    Petitioner for dew ;
No Saxon spade disturb'd his root,
The rabbit spared the tender shoot,
    And valiantly he grew,

And show'd some inches from the ground
When St. Augustine came and found
    Us very proper Vandals :

Then nymphs had bluer eyes than hose.
England then measured men by blows,
    And measured time by candles.

The pilgrim bless'd his grateful shade
Ere Richard led the first crusade ;
    And maidens loved to dance
Where, boy and man, in summer-time,
Chaucer once ponder'd o'er his rhyme ;
    And Robin Hood, perchance,

Stole hither to Maid Marian ;
(And if they did not come, one can
    At any rate suppose it) ;
They met beneath the mistletoe,—
We've done the same, and ought to know
    The reason why they chose it !

And   this   was   call'd   the   *Traitor's*
        Branch,
Guy Warwick hung six yeomen stanch
    Along its mighty fork ;   .
Uncivil wars for them !   The fair
Red rose and white still bloom, but
        where
    Are Lancaster and York ?

Right mournfully his leaves he shed
To shroud the graves of England's dead,
　　By English falchion slain ;
And cheerfully, for England's sake,
He sent his kin to sea with Drake,
　　When Tudor humbled Spain.

While Blake was fighting with the Dutch
They gave his poor old arms a crutch ;
　　And thrice four maids and men ate
A meal within his rugged bark,
When Coventry bewitch'd the Park,
　　And Chatham swayed the Senate.

His few remaining boughs were green,
And dappled sunbeams danced between
　　Upon the dappled deer,
When, clad in black, two mourners met
To read the Waterloo Gazette,—
　　They mourn'd their darling here.

They join'd their boy.　The tree at last
Lies prone, discoursing of the past,
　　Some fancy-dreams awaking ;
At rest, though headlong changes come,

Though nations arm to roll of drum,
   And dynasties are quaking.

Romantic spot! By honest pride
Of old tradition sanctified;
   My pensive vigil keeping,
Thy beauty moves me like a spell,
And thoughts, and tender thoughts, up-
    well,
   That fill my heart to weeping.

  *   *   *   *   *

The Squire affirms with gravest look,
His Oak goes up to Domesday Book:
   And some say even higher!
We rode last week to see the Ruin,
We love the fair domain it grew in,
   And well we love the Squire.

A nature loyally controlled,
And fashion'd in that righteous mould
   Of English gentleman;
My child some day will read these
   rhymes,
She loved her " godpapa " betimes,—
   The little Christian!

I love the Past, its ripe pleasânce,
And lusty thought, and dim romance,—
   Its heart-compelling ditties ;
But more, these ties, in mercy sent,
With faith and true affection blent,
And, wanting them, I were content
   To murmur, " *Nunc dimittis.*"

HALLINGBURY : *April,* 1859.

TO MY GRANDMOTHER.

(SUGGESTED BY A PICTURE BY MR.
ROMNEY.)

Under the elm a rustic seat
Was merriest Susan's pet retreat
To merry make.

THIS relative of mine,
Was she seventy-and-nine
    When she died?
By the canvas may be seen
How she look'd at seventeen,
    As a bride.

Beneath a summer tree,
Her maiden reverie
    Has a charm ;
Her ringlets are in taste ;
What an arm ! . . what a waist
    For an arm !

With her bridal-wreath, bouquet,
Lace farthingale, and gay
    Falbala,—
Were Romney's limning true,
What a lucky dog were you,
    Grandpapa !

Her lips are sweet as love ;
They are parting !   Do they move ?
    Are they dumb ?
Her eyes are blue, and beam
Beseechingly, and seem
    To say, " Come ! "

What funny fancy slips
From atween these cherry lips ?
    Whisper me,
Sweet sorceress in paint,
What canon says I mayn't
    Marry thee ?

That good-for-nothing Time
Has a confidence sublime !
    When I first
Saw this lady, in my youth,

Her winters had, forsooth,
    Done their worst.

Her locks, as white as snow,
Once shamed the swarthy crow :
    By-and-by
That fowl's avenging sprite
Set his cruel foot for spite
    Near her eye.

Her rounded form was lean,
And her silk was bombazine :
    Well I wot
With her needles would she sit,
And for hours would she knit,—
    Would she not ?

Ah, perishable clay ;
Her charms had dropt away
    One by one :
But if she heaved a sigh
With a burthen, it was, " Thy
    Will be done."

In travail, as in tears,
With the fardel of her years

Overprest,
In mercy she was borne
Where the weary and the worn
    Are at rest.

O, if you now are there,
And sweet as once you were,
    Grandmamma,
This nether world agrees
'Twill all the better please
    Grandpapa.

THE SKELETON IN THE CUP-
BOARD.

The most forlorn—what worms we are!
Would wish to finish this cigar
Before departing.

THE characters of great and small
    Come ready made, we can't bespeak
        one ;
Their sides are many, too,—and all
    (Except ourselves) have got a weak
        one.
Some sanguine people love for life,
    Some love their hobby till it flings
        them.—
How many love a pretty wife
    For love of the *éclat* she brings them !

A little to relieve my mind
    I've thrown off this disjointed chatter,
But more because I'm disinclined
    To enter on a painful matter :

Once I was bashful; I'll allow
   I've blush'd for words untimely
     spoken;
I still am rather shy, and now . . .
   And now the ice is fairly broken.

We all have secrets : you have one
   Which mayn't be quite your charm-
     ing spouse's ;
We all lock up a skeleton
   In some grim chamber of our houses ;
Familiars who exhaust their days
   And nights in probing where our
     smart is—
And who, excepting spiteful ways,
   Are " silent, unassuming *parties.*"

We hug this phantom we detest,
   Rarely we let it cross our portals:
It is a most exacting guest,—
   Now, are we not afflicted mortals ?
Your neighbour Gay, that jovial wight,
   As Dives rich, and brave as Hector—
Poor Gay steals twenty times a night,
   On shaking knees, to see his spectre.

Old Dives fears a pauper fate,
  So hoarding in his ruling passion ;—
Some gloomy souls anticipate
  A waistcoat, straiter than the fash·
    ion !—
She childless pines, that lonely wife,
  And secret tears are bitter shed·
    ding ;—
Hector may tremble all his life,
  And die,—but not of that he's dread-
    ing.

Ah me, the World ! How fast it spins !
  The beldams dance, the caldron bub·
    bles ;
They shriek,—they stir it for our sins,
  And we must drain it for our troubles.
We toil, we groan ;—the cry for love
  Mounts up from this poor seething
    city,
And yet I know we have above
  A FATHER, infinite in pity.

When Beauty smiles, when Sorrow
  weeps,

Where sunbeams play, where shadows
    darken,
One inmate of our dwelling keeps
    Its ghastly carnival ;—but hearken !
How dry the rattle of the bones !
    That sound was not to make you start
        meant :
Stand by ! Your humble servant owns
    The Tenant of this Dark Apartment.

ON AN OLD MUFF.

He cannot be complete in aught
Who is not humorously prone,—
A man without a merry thought
Can hardly have a funny bone.

TIME has a magic wand!
What is this meets my hand,
Moth-eaten, mouldy, and
    Cover'd with fluff?
Faded, and stiff, and scant;
Can it be? no, it can't—
Yes, I declare, it's Aunt
    Prudence's Muff!

Years ago, twenty-three,
Old Uncle Doubledee
Gave it to Aunty P.
    Laughing and teasing—
" Pru., of the breezy curls,
Question those solemn churls,
What holds a pretty girl's
    Hand without squeezing? "

Uncle was then a lad
Gay, but, I grieve to add,
Sinful ; if smoking bad
   Baccy's vice :
Glossy was then this mink
Muff, lined with pretty pink
Satin, which maidens think
   " Awfully nice ! "

I seem to see again
Aunt in her hood and train,
Glide, with a sweet disdain,
   Gravely to Meeting :
Psalm-book, and kerchief new,
Peep'd from the Muff of Pru.;
Young men, and pious too,
   Giving her greeting.

Sweetly her Sabbath sped
Then ; from this Muff, it's said,
Tracts she distributed :—
   Converts (till Monday !)
Lured by the grace they lack'd,
Follow'd her.   One, in fact,
Ask'd for—and got his tract
   Twice of a Sunday !

Love has a potent spell ;
Soon this bold *Ne'er-do-well*,
Aunt's too susceptible
    Heart undermining,
Slipt, so the scandal runs,
Notes in the pretty nun's
Muff, triple-corner'd ones,
    Pink as its lining.

Worse follow'd, soon the jade
Fled (to oblige her blade !)
Whilst her friends thought that they'd
    Lock'd her up tightly :
After such shocking games
Aunt is of wedded dames
Gayest, and now her name's
    Mrs. Golightly.

In female conduct flaw
Sadder I never saw,
Faith still I've in the law
    Of compensation.
Once Uncle went astray,
Smoked, joked, and swore away,
Sworn by he's now, by a
    Large congregation.

Changed is the Child of Sin,
Now he's (he once was thin)
Grave, with a double chin,—
    Blest be his fat form !
Changed is the garb he wore,
Preacher was never more
Prized than is Uncle for
    Pulpit or platform.

If all's as best befits
Mortals of slender wits,
Then beg this Muff and its
    Fair Owner pardon :
All's for the best, indeed
Such is My simple creed ;
Still I must go and weed
    Hard in my garden.

1863.

AN INVITATION TO ROME, AND THE REPLY.

THE INVITATION.

OH, come to Rome, it is a pleasant
  place,
  Your London sun is here, and smiling
  brightly;
The Briton, too, puts on his cheery face,
And Mrs. Bull acquits herself politely.
The Romans are an easy-going race,
  With simple wives more dignified
  than sprightly;
I see them at their doors, as day is
  closing,
Prouder than duchesses, and more im-
  posing.

A sweet *far niente* life promotes the
  graces;

They pass from dreamy bliss to wake-
    ful glee,
And in their bearing and their speech,
    one traces
A breadth, a depth—a grace of cour-
    tesy
Not found in busy or inclement places ;
    Their clime and tongue are much in
    harmony :—
The Cockney met in Middlesex or Surrey,
Is often cold, and always in a hurry.

Oh, come to Rome, nor be content to
    read
Of famous palace and of stately street
Whose fountains ever run with joyful
    speed,
And never-ceasing murmur. Here
    we greet
Memnon's vast monolith ; or, gay with
    weed,
    Rich capitals, as corner-stone, or seat,
The site of vanish'd temples, where now
    moulder
Old ruins, masking ruin even older.

Ay, come, and see the statues, pictures,
    churches,
  Although the last are commonplace,
    or florid.—
Who say 'tis here that superstition
    perches ?
  Myself, I'm glad the marbles have
    been quarried.
The sombre streets are worthy your re-
    searches :
  The ways are foul, the lava pavement's
    horrid,
But pleasant sights that squeamishness
    disparages,
Are miss'd by all who roll about in car-
    riages.

I dare not speak of Michael Angelo,
  Such theme were all too splendid for
    my pen :
And if I breathe the name of Sanzio
  (The brightest of Italian gentlemen,)
Is it that love casts out my fear, and so
  I claim with him a kindredship ? Ah,
    when

We love, the name is on our hearts en-
graven,
As is thy name, my own dear Bard of
Avon.

Nor is the Coliseum theme of mine,
   'Twas built for poet of a larger daring ;
The world goes there with torches ; I
   decline
      Thus to affront the moonbeams with
      their flaring.
Some time in May our forces we'll com-
   bine
      (Just you and I), and try a midnight
      airing.
And then I'll quote this rhyme to you—
   and then
You'll muse upon the vanity of men !

Come !   We will charter such a pair of
   nags !
   The country's better seen when one is
   riding :
We'll roam where yellow Tiber speeds
   or lags

At will. The aqueducts are yet be-
striding
With giant march (now whole, now broken crags
With flowers plumed) the swelling
and subsiding
Campagna, girt by purple hills afar,
That melt in light beneath the evening
star.

A drive to Palestrina will be pleasant ;
The wild fig grows where erst her
rampart stood ;
There oft, in goat-skin clad, a sunburnt
peasant
Like Pan comes frisking from his ilex
wood,
And seems to wake the past time in the
present.
Fair *contadina*, mark his mirthful
mood,
No antique satyr he. The nimble fellow
Can join with jollity your *saltarello*.

Old sylvan peace and liberty! The
    breath
Of life to unsophisticated man.
Here Mirth may pipe, Love here may
    weave his wreath,
  " Per dar' al mio bene." When you
    can,
Come share their leafy solitudes. Pale
    Death
And Time are grudging of our little
    span :
Wan Time speeds lightly o'er the
    changing corn,
Death grins from yonder cynical old
    thorn.
Oh, come! I send a leaf of April
    fern,
It grew where beauty lingers round
    decay :
Ashes long buried in a sculptured urn
  Are not more dead than Rome—so
    dead to-day !
That better time, for which the patriots
    yearn,
Delights the gaze, again to fade away.

They wait, they pine for what is long
    denied,
And thus I wait till thou art by my side.

Thou'rt far away! Yet, while I write, I
    still
  Seem gently, Sweet, to clasp thy
      hand in mine ;
I cannot bring myself to drop the quill,
  I cannot yet thy little hand resign !
The plain is fading into darkness chill,
  The Sabine peaks are flushed with
      light divine,
I watch alone, my fond thought wings
    to thee ;
Oh, come to Rome.   Oh come,—oh
    come to me !

  1863.

———————————

THE REPLY.

Dear Exile, I was proud to get
  Your rhyme, I've laid it up in cotton ;
You know that you are all to " Pet,"—
  She fear'd that she was quite forgotten.

Mamma, who scolds me when I mope,
 Insists, and she is wise as gentle,
That I am still in love! I hope
 That you feel rather sentimental!

Perhaps you think your *Love forlore*
 Should pine unless her slave be with
  her.
Of course you're fond of Rome, and
  more—
 Of course you'd like to coax me
  thither!
Che! quit this dear, delightful maze
 Of calls and balls, to be intensely
Discomfited in fifty ways—
 I like your confidence, immensely!

Some girls who love to ride and race,
 And live for dancing, like the Bruens,
Confess that Rome's a charming place—
 In spite of all the stupid ruins!
I think it might be sweet to pitch
 One's tent beside those banks of
  Tiber,
And all that sort of thing, of which

Dear Hawthorne's "quite" the best
describer.

To see stone pines and marble gods
   In garden alleys red with roses ;—
The Perch where Pio Nono nods ;—
   The Church where Raphael reposes.
Make pleasant *giros*—when we may;
   Jump *stagionate* (where they're easy !)
And play croquet ; the Bruens say
   There's turf behind the Ludovici !

I'll bring my books, though Mrs. Mee
   Says packing books is such a worry ;
I'll bring my *Golden Treasury*,
   Manzoni, and, of course, a " Mur-
     ray ! "
Your verses (if you so advise !)
   A Dante—Auntie owns a quarto ;
I'll try and buy a smaller size,
   And read him on the *muro torto*.

But can I go ?   *La Madre* thinks
   It would be such an undertaking !
(I wish we could consult a sphinx !)

The thought alone has left her quak-
　　ing !
Papa (we do not mind papa)
　　Has got some " notice " of some
　　" motion,"
And could not stay ; but, why not,—ah,
　　I've not the very slightest notion !

The Browns have come to stay a week—
　　They've brought the boys—I haven't
　　　thank'd 'em ;
For Baby *Grand*, and Baby *Pic*,
　　Are playing cricket in my sanctum !
Your Rover, too, affects my den,
　　And when I pat the dear old whelp,
　　　it　.　.
It makes me think of *You*, and then　.　.
　　And then I cry—I cannot help it.

Ah yes, before you left me, ere
　　Our separation was impending,
These eyes had seldom shed a tear,—
　　I thought my joy could have no end-
　　　ing !
But cloudlets gather'd soon, and this —

This was the first that rose to grieve
    me—
To know that I possess'd the bliss,—
    For then I knew such bliss might
    leave me!

My strain is sad, but, oh, believe
    Your words have made my spirit
    better;
And if, perhaps, at times I grieve,
    I'd meant to write a cheery letter;
But skies were dull; Rome sounded hot,
    I fancied I could live without it:
I thought I'd go, I thought I'd not,
    And then I thought I'd think about it.

The sun now glances o'er the Park,
    If tears are on my cheek, they glitter,
I think I've kissed your rhyme, for hark,
    My "bulley" gives a saucy twitter!
Your blessed words extinguish doubt,
    A sudden breeze is gaily blowing,—
And Hark! The minster bells ring out—
    *She ought to go. Of course she's
    going!*
1863.

GERALDINE.

She will not need the Shepherd's crook,
Her griefs are only passing shadow ;
She'll bask beside the purest brook,
And nibble in the greenest meadow.

A SIMPLE child has claims
On your sentiment, her name's
    Geraldine.
Be tender, but beware,
She's frolicsome as fair,—
    And fifteen.

She has gifts to grace allied,
And each she has applied,
    And improved :
She has bliss that lives and leans
On loving,—ah, that means
    She is loved.

Her beauty is refined
By sweet harmony of mind.

And the art,
And the blessed nature, too,
Of a tender, of a true
    Little heart.

And yet I must not vault
Over any foolish fault
    That she owns ;
Or others might rebel,
And enviously swell
    In their zones.

For she's tricksy as the fays,
Or her pussy when it plays
    With a string :
She's a goose about her cat,
Her ribbons, and all that
    Sort of thing.

These foibles are a blot,
Still she never can do what
    Is not *nice ;*
Such as quarrel, and give slaps—
As I've known her get, perhaps,
    Once or twice.

The spells that draw her soul
Are subtle—sad or droll :
　　She can show
That virtuoso whim
Which consecrates our dim
　　Long-ago.

A love that is not sham
For Stothard, Blake, and Lamb ;
　　And I've known
Cordelia's sad eyes
Cause angel-tears to rise
　　In her own.

Her gentle spirit yearns
When she reads of Robin Burns ;—
　　Luckless Bard,
Had she blossom'd in thy time,
Oh, how rare had been the rhyme
　　—And reward !

Thrice happy then is he
Who, planting such a Tree,
　　Sees it bloom
To shelter him ; indeed

We have joyance as we speed
　　To our doom !

I am happy, having grown
Such a Sapling of my own ;
　　And I crave
No garland for my brows,
But rest beneath its boughs
　　To the grave.

1864.

THE HOUSEMAID.

The poor can love through toil and pain,
Although their homely speech is fain
To halt in fetters :
They feel as much, and do far more
Than some of those they bow before,
Miscall'd their betters.

WISTFUL she stands—and yet resign'd
She watches by the window-blind :
   Poor girl. No doubt
The pilgrims here despise thy lot :
Thou canst not stir, because 'tis not
   Thy *Sunday out.*

To play a game of hide and seek
With dust and cobweb all the week
   Small pleasure yields :
Oh dear, how nice it is to drop
One's pen and ink—one's pail and mop :
   And scour the fields.

Poor Bodies few such pleasures know ;
Seldom they come. How soon they go !

But Souls can roam ;
For lapt in visions airy-sweet,
She sees in this unlovely street
　　Her far-off home.

The street is now no street ! She pranks
A purling brook with thymy banks.
　　In fancy's realm
Yon post supports no lamp, aloof
It spreads above her parents' roof,—
　　A gracious elm.

A father's aid, a mother's care,
And life for her was happy there :
　　Yet here, in thrall
She　sits,　and　dreams,　and　fondly
　　dreams,
And fondly smiles on one who seems
　　More dear than all.

Her dwelling-place I can't disclose!
Suppose her fair, her name suppose
　　Is *Car*, or *Kitty ;*
She　may　be　*Jane* — she　might　be
　　plain—

For must the subject of my strain
    Be always pretty ?
      *   *   *

Oft on a cloudless afternoon
Of budding May and leafy June,
    Fit Sunday weather,
I pass thy window by design,
And wish thy Sunday out and mine
    Might fall together.

For sweet it were thy lot to dower
With one brief joy : a white-robed flower
    That prude or preacher
Hardly could deem it were unmeet
To lay on thy poor path, thou sweet,
    Forlorn, young creature.
      *   *   *

But if her thought on wooing run
And if her Sunday-swain is one
    Who's fond of strolling,
She'd like my nonsense less than his
And so it's better as it is—
    And that's consoling.

  1864.

THE JESTER'S PLEA.

These verses were published in 1862, in a volume of
Poems (by several hands), entitled "An Offering to
Lancashire."

THE world's a sorry wench, akin
  To all that's frail and frightful:
The world's as ugly, ay, as sin,—
  And almost as delightful!
The world's a merry world (*pro tem.*),
  And some are gay, and therefore
It pleases them, but some condemn
  The world they do not care for.

The world's an ugly world. Offend
  Good people, how they wrangle!
Their manners that they never mend,—
  The characters they mangle!
They eat, and drink, and scheme, and
    plod,—
  They go to church on Sunday;

And many are afraid of God—
And more of *Mrs. Grundy*.

The time for pen and sword was when
" My ladye fayre " for pity
Could tend her wounded knight, and
then
Be tender to his ditty.
Some ladies now make pretty songs,
And some make pretty nurses :
Some men are great at righting wrongs,
And some at writing verses.

I wish we better understood
The tax our poets levy ;
I know the Muse is *goody good*,
I think she's rather heavy :
Now she compounds for winning ways
By morals of the sternest ;
Methinks the lays of nowadays
Are painfully in earnest.

When wisdom halts, I humbly try
To make the most of folly :
If Pallas be unwilling, I

Prefer to flirt with Polly ;
To quit the goddess for the maid
    Seems low in lofty musers ;
But Pallas is a lofty jade—
    And beggars can't be choosers.

I do not wish to see the slaves
    Of party stirring passion,
Or psalms quite superseding staves
    Or piety " the fashion."
I bless the Hearts where pity glows,
    Who, here together banded,
Are holding out a hand to those
    That wait so empty-handed !

Masters, may one in motley clad,
    A Jester by confession,
Scarce noticed join, half gay, half sad,
    The close of your procession ?
This garment here seems out of place
    With graver robes to mingle,
But if one tear bedews his face,
    Forgive the bells their jingle.

TO MY MISTRESS.

His musings were trite, and their burden, forsooth,
The wisdom of age and the folly of youth.

COUNTESS, I see the flying year,
And feel how Time is wasting here :
Ay more, he soon his worst will do,
And garner all Your roses too.

It pleases Time to fold his wings
Around our best and fairest things ;
He'll mar your blooming cheek, as now
He stamps his mark upon my brow.

The same mute planets rise and shine
To rule your days and nights as mine :
Once I was young and gay, and
      see ! . .
What I am now you soon will be.

And yet I boast a certain charm
That shields me from your worst alarm ;

And bids me gaze, with front sublime,
On all these ravages of Time.

You boast a gift to charm the eyes,
I boast a gift that Time defies :
For mine will still be mine, and last
When all your pride of beauty's past.

My gift may long embalm the lures
Of eyes—ah, sweet to me as yours :
For ages hence the great and good
Will judge you as I choose they should.

In days to come the peer or clown,
With whom I still shall win renown,
Will only know that you were fair
Because I chanced to say you were

Proud Lady! Scornful beauty mocks
At aged heads and silver locks ;
But think awhile before you fly,
Or spurn a poet such as I.

KENWOOD : *July* 21, 1864.

MY MISTRESS'S BOOTS.

She has dancing eyes and ruby lips,
Delightful boots—and away she skips.

THEY nearly strike me dumb,—
I tremble when they come
    Pit-a-pat :
This palpitation means
These boots are Geraldine's—
    Think of that !

O, where did hunter win
So delicate a skin
    For her feet ?
You lucky little kid,
You perish'd, so you did,
    For my sweet.

The faery stitching gleams
On the sides, and in the seams,
    And it shows

The Pixies were the wags
Who tipt these funny tags,
  And these toes.

What soles to charm an elf!
Had Crusoe, sick of self,
  Chanced to view
One printed near the tide,
O, how hard he would have tried
  For the two!

For Gerry's debonair,
And innocent and fair
  As a rose ;
She's an angel in a frock,
She's an angel with a clock
  To her hose.

The simpletons who squeeze
Their extremities to please
  Mandarins,
Would positively flinch
From venturing to pinch
  Geraldine's.

Cinderalla's *lefts and rights*
To Geraldine's were frights :
   And I trow,
The damsel, deftly shod,
Has dutifully trod
   Until now.

Come, Gerry, since it suits
Such a pretty Puss (in Boots)
   These to don,
Set this dainty hand awhile
On my shoulder, dear, and I'll
   Put them on.

ALBURY, *June* 29, 1864.

THE ROSE AND THE RING.

(Christmas, 1854, and Christmas, 1863.)

SHE smiles, but her heart is in sable,
  Ay, sad as her Christmas is chill;
She reads, and her book is the fable
  He penn'd for her while she was ill.
It is nine years ago since he wrought it,
  Where reedy old Tiber is king;
And chapter by chapter he brought it,
  And read her the Rose and the Ring.

And when it was printed, and gaining
  Renown with all lovers of glee,
He sent her this copy containing
  His comical little *croquis;*
A sketch of a rather droll couple—
  She's pretty, he's quite t'other thing!
He begs (with a spine vastly supple)
  She will study the Rose and the Ring.

It pleased the kind Wizard to send her
  The last and the best of his toys;
He aye had a sentiment tender
  For innocent maidens and boys;
And though he was great as a scorner,
  The guileless were safe from his
    sting :—
How sad is past mirth to the mourner—
  A tear on the Rose and the Ring !

She reads; I may vainly endeavour
  Her mirth-chequer'd grief to pursue,
For she knows she has lost, and for ever,
  The heart that was bared to so few;
But here, on the shrine of his glory,
  One poor little blossom I fling;
And you see there's a nice little story
  Attach'd to the Rose and the Ring.

  1864.

NUPTIAL VERSES.

THE town despises new world lays :
  The foolish town is frantic
For story-books that tell of days
  Which time has made romantic ;
Of days, whose chiefest glories fill
  The gloom of crypt and barrow ;
When soldiers were, as Love is still,
  Content with bow and arrow.

But why should we the fancy chide ?
  The world will always hunger
To know how people lived and died
  When all the world was younger.
We like to read of knightly parts
  In maidenhood's distresses,
Of tryst, with sunshine in light hearts,
  And moonbeam on dark tresses ;

And how, when *errante-knyghte* or *erl*
  Proved well the love he gave her,

She'd send him scarf or silken curl,
    As earnest of her favour;
And how (the Fair at times were rude!)
    Her knight, ere homeward riding,
Would take, and, ay with gratitude,
    His lady's silver chiding.

We love the rare old days and rich
    That poetry has painted;
We mourn that sacred age with which
    We never were acquainted.
Absurd! our modern world's divine,
    A world to dare and do in,
A more romantic world.   In fine
    A better world to woo in!

The flow of life is yet a rill
    That laughs, and leaps, and glistens;
And still the woodland rings, and still
    The old Damœtas listens.
Romance, as tender as she's true,
    Our Isle has never quitted:
So, LAD and LASSIE, when you woo,
    You hardly need be pitied.

Our lot is cast on pleasant days,
   In not unpleasant places ;
Young ladies now have pretty ways,
   As well as pretty faces ;
So never sigh for what has been,
   And let us cease complaining
That we have loved when our dear
     Queen
   VICTORIA was reigning.

Oh yes, young love is lovely yet,
   With faith and honour plighted :
I love to see a pair so met,
   Youth—Beauty—all united.
Such dear ones may they ever wear
   The roses fortune gave them:
Ah, know we such a BLESSED PAIR ?
   I think we do ! GOD SAVE THEM !

MRS. SMITH.

Heigh ho ! they're wed. The cards are dealt,
Our frolic games are o'er ;
I've laugh'd, and fool'd, and loved. I've felt—
As I shall feel no more ;
Yon little thatch is where she lives,
Yon spire is where she met me ;—
I think that if she quite forgives,
She cannot quite forget me.

LAST year I trod these fields with Di,
Fields fresh with clover and with rye ;
   Now they seem arid.
Then Di was fair and single ; how
Unfair it seems on me, for now
   Di's fair—and married !

A blissful swain—I scorn'd the song
Which says that though young Love is
     strong,
   The Fates are stronger:
Breezes then blew a boon to men,
The buttercups were bright, and then
   This grass was longer.

That day I saw and much esteem'd
Di's ankles, which the clover seem'd
    Inclined to smother:
It twitch'd, and soon untied (for fun)
The ribbon of her shoes, first one,
    And then the other.

I'm told that virgins augur some
Misfortune if their shoe-strings come
    To grief on Friday:
And so did Di, and then her pride
Decreed that shoe-strings so untied
    Are "so untidy!"

Of course I knelt; with fingers deft
I tied the right, and tied the left:
    Says Di, "The stubble
Is very stupid!—as I live
I'm quite ashamed! . . . I'm shock'd
    to give
    You so much trouble!"

For answer I was fain to sink
To what we all would say and think
    Were Beauty present:

" Don't mention such a simple act—
A trouble ? not the least !   In fact
    It's rather pleasant ! "

I trust that Love will never tease
Poor little Di, or prove that he's
    A graceless rover.
She's happy now as *Mrs. Smith*—
And less polite when walking with
    Her chosen lover !

Heigh-ho !   Although no moral clings
To Di's blue eyes, and sandal strings,
    We've had our quarrels.
I think that Smith is thought an ass,—
I know that when they walk in grass
    She wears *balmorals.*

  1864.

IMPLORA PACE.

My lot as I rove,
  Is to sing for the throng;
And will not they love
  The poor child for his song?

LIFE is at best a weary round
  Of mingled joy and woe ;
How soon the passing knell will sound !
  Is death a friend or foe ?
Our fleeting days are sad, and vain
Is much that tempts us to remain
  Yet we are loth to go.
Must I soon tread yon silent shore,
Go hence, and then be seen no more ?

I love to think that those I loved
  May gather round the bier
Of him who, if he erring proved,
  Still held them more than dear.
My friends grow fewer day by day,
Yes, one by one they drop away ;

And if I shed no tear,
Departed shades, while life endures,
This poor heart yearns for love—and
    Yours.

That day, will there be one to shed
    A tear behind the hearse ?
Or cry, " Poor *Yorick*, are you dead ?
    I could have spared a worse—
We never spoke ; we never met ;
I never heard your voice ; and yet
    I loved you for your verse ? "
Such love would make the flowers wave
In gladness on their poet's grave.

A few, few years, like one short week,
    Will pass and leave behind
A stone moss-grown, that none will
    seek,
    And none would care to find.
Then I shall sleep, and gain release
In perfect rest—the perfect peace
    For which my soul has pined ;—
And men will love, and weary men
Will sue for quiet slumber then.

MR. PLACID'S FLIRTATION.

" Jemima was cross, and I lost my umbrella
That day at the tomb of Cecilia Metella."

MISS TRISTRAM'S *poulet* ended thus :
"Nota bene,
We meet for croquet in the Aldobran-
dini."
Says my wife, "Then I'll drive, and
you'll ride with Selina"
(Jones's fair spouse, of the Via Sistina).

We started : I'll own that my family
deem
I'm an ass, but I'm not such an ass as I
seem ;
As we crossed the stones gently a nurse-
maid said " La—
There goes Mrs. Jones with Miss Placid's
papa!"

Our friends, one or two may be men-
    tion'd anon,
Had arranged *rendezvous* at the Gate
    of St. John :
That pass'd, off we spun over turf that's
    not green there,
And soon were all met at the villa.
    You've been there ?

I'll try and describe, or I won't, if you
    please,
The cheer that was set for us under the
    trees :
You have read the *menu*, may you read
    it again ;
Champagne, perigord, galantine, and—
    champagne.

Suffice it to say, I got seated between
Mrs. Jones and old Brown—to the lat-
    ter's chagrin.
Poor Brown, who believes in himself,
    and—another thing,
Whose talk is so bald, but whose cheeks
    are so—t'other thing.

She sang, her sweet voice fill'd the gay
    garden alleys ;
I jested, but Brown would not smile at
    my sallies ;—
Selina remark'd that a swell met at
    Rome
Is not always a swell when you meet
    him at home.

The luncheon despatch'd, we adjourn'd
    to croquet,
A dainty, but difficult sport in its way.
Thus I counsel the sage, who to play at
    it stoops,
Belabour thy neighbour, and spoon
    through thy hoops.

Then we stroll'd, and discourse found
    its kindest of tones :
" Oh, how charming were solitude and
    —Mrs. Jones ! "
" Indeed, Mr. Placid, I dote on the
    sheeny
And shadowy paths of the Aldobran-
    dini !

A girl came with violet posies, and two
Gentle eyes, like her violets, freshen'd
    with dew,
And a kind of an indolent, fine-lady
    air,—
As if she by accident found herself there.

I bought one.   Selina was pleased to ac-
    cept it;
She gave me a rosebud to keep—and
    I've kept it.
Then twilight was near, and I think, in
    my heart,
When she vow'd she must go, she was
    loth to depart.

Cattivo momento! we dare not delay:
The steeds are remounted, and wheels
    roll away:
The ladies *condemn* Mrs. Jones, as the
    phrase is,
But vie with each other in chanting my
    praises.

"He has so much to say!" cries the
    fair Mrs. Legge;

" How amusing he wás about missing
    the peg ! "
" What a beautiful smile !" says the
    plainest Miss Gunn.
All echo, " He's charming ! delightful!
    —What fun !"

This sounds rather *nice*, and it's per-
    fectly clear it
Had sounded more *nice* had I happen'd
    to hear it ;
The men were less civil, and gave me a
    rub,
So I happen'd to hear when I went to
    the Club.

Says Brown, "I shall drop Mr. Placid's
    society ; "
(Brown is a prig of improper propriety ;)
" Hang him," said Smith (who from
    cant's not exempt),
" Why he'll bring immorality into con-
    tempt."

Says I (to myself) when I found me
    alone,

" My dear wife has my heart, is it always her own ? "
And further, says I (to myself), " I'll be
shot
If I know if Selina adores me or not."

Says Jones, " I've just come from the
scavi, at Veii,
And I've brought some remarkably fine
scarabæi ! "

BEGGARS.

Some beggars look on: I extremely regret it—
They wish for a taste. Don't they wish they may
*   get it.*
She thus aggravates both the humble and needy,—
You'll own she is thoughtless—I think she is greedy.
                                        PUNCH.

I AM pacing the Mall in a rapt reverie,—
I am thinking if Sophy is thinking of me,
When I'm roused by a ragged and
      shivering wretch,
Who seems to be well on his way to
      Jack Ketch.

He has got a bad face, and a shocking
      bad hat ;
A comb in his fist, and he sees I'm a
      flat,
For he says, " Buy a comb, it's a fine
      un to wear ;
On'y try it, my Lord, through your whis-
      kers and 'air."

He eyes my gold chain, as if anxious to
    crib it ;
He looks just as if he'd been blown from
    a gibbet.
I pause . . . I pass on, and beside
    the club fire
I settle that Sophy is all I desire.

As I walk from the club, and am deep
    in a strophè
That rolls upon all that's delicious in
    Sophy,
I'm humbly address'd by an "object"
    unnerving,
So tatter'd a wretch must be "highly
    deserving."

She begs,—I am touch'd, but I've great
    circumspection :
I stifle remorse with the soothing reflec-
    tion
That cases of vice are by no means a
    rarity—
The worst vice of all's indiscriminate
    charity.

Am I right ?   How I wish that my cleri-
    cal guide
Would settle this question—and others
    beside.
For always one's heart to be hardening
    thus,
If wholesome for beggars, is hurtful for
    us.

A few minutes later I'm happy and
    free
To sip " *Its own Sophykins'* " five-
    o'clock tea :
Her table is loaded, for when a girl
    marries,
What bushels of rubbish they send her
    from *Barry's !*

" There's a present for you, Sir !" Yes,
    thanks to her thrift,
My Pet has been able to buy me a gift ;
And she slips in my hand, the delight-
    fully sly Thing,
A paper-weight form'd of a bronze lizard
    writhing.

"What a charming *cadeau!* and so
    truthfully moulded ;
But perhaps you don't know, or deserve
    to be scolded,
That in casting this metal a live, harm-
    less lizard
Was cruelly tortured in ghost and in
    gizzard ? "

" Po-oh ! "—says my lady, (she always
    says " Pooh "
When she's wilful, and does what she
    oughtn't to do !)
" Hopgarten protests they've no feeling,
    and so
It was only their *muscular movement*,
    you know ! "

Thinks I (when I've said *au revoir*, and
    depart—
A Comb in my pocket, a Weight—at
    my heart),
And when wretched mendicants writhe,
    there's a notion
That begging is only their " muscular
    motion."

THE JESTER'S MORAL.

I grudge that lonely man his crook,
It seems no idle whim
That if he reads in Nature's book,
Her voice has been to him
A spiritual life, to sway
And cheer him on his endless way.

THE OLD SHEPHERD.

Is human life a pleasant game
    That gives the palm to all?
A fight for fortune, or for fame,
    A struggle, and a fall?
Who views the Past, and all he prized,
    With tranquil exultation?
And who can say—I've realised
    My fondest aspiration?

Alas, not one. No, rest assured
    That all are prone to quarrel
With fate, when worms destroy their
        gourd,
    Or mildew spoils their laurel :

The prize may come to cheer our lot,
   But all too late ; and granted
If even better, still it's not
   Exactly what we wanted.

My schoolboy time !   I wish to praise
   That bud of brief existence,—
The vision of my younger days
   Now trembles in the distance.
An envious vapour lingers here,
   And there I find a chasm ;
But much remains, distinct and clear,
   To sink enthusiasm.

Such thoughts just now disturb my soul
   With reason good, for lately
I took the train to Marley-knoll,
   And cross'd the fields to Mately.
I found old Wheeler at his gate,
   He once rare sport could show me :
My Mentor too on springe and bait—
   But Wheeler did not know me.

" Goodlord ! " at last exclaim'd the
      churl,
   " Are you the little chap, sir,

What used to train his hair in curl,
  And wore a scarlet cap, sir ? "
And then he took to fill in blanks,
  And conjure up old faces ;
And talk of well-remember'd pranks
  In half-forgotten places.

It pleased the man to tell his brief
  And rather mournful story,—
Old Bliss's school had come to grief,
  And Bliss had " gone to glory."
Fell'd were his trees, his house was
        razed,
  And what less keenly pain'd me,
A venerable donkey grazed
  Exactly where he caned me.

And where have all my playmates sped,
  Whose ranks were once so serried?
Why some are wed, and some are dead,
  And some are only buried ;
Frank Petre, then so full of fun,
  Is now St. Blaise's prior,
And Travers, the attorney's son
  Is member for the shire.

Dull maskers we—Life's festival
  Enchants the blithe new-comer ;
But seasons change ;—oh where are all
  Those friendships of our summer ?
Wan pilgrims flit athwart our track,
  Cold looks attend the meeting ;
We only greet them, glancing back,
  Or pass without a greeting.

Old Bliss I owe some rubs, but pride
  Constrains me to postpone 'em,—
Something he taught me, ere he died,
  About *nil nisi bonum.*
I've met with wiser, better men,
  But I forgive him wholly ;
Perhaps his jokes were sad, but then
  He used to storm so drolly.

" I still can laugh " is still my boast,
  But mirth has sounded gayer ;
And which provokes my laughter most,
  The preacher or the player ?
Alack, I cannot laugh at what
  Once made us laugh so freely ;
For Nestroy and Grassot are not—
  And where is Mr. Keeley ?

I'll join St. Blaise (a verseman fit,
　More fit than I, once did it)
—*I* shave my crown ?   No, Common
　　Wit
And Common Sense forbid it.
I'd sooner dress your Little Miss
　As Paulet shaves his poodles !
As soon propose for Betsy Bliss,
　Or get proposed for Boodle's.

We prate of Life's illusive dyes,
　And yet fond Hope misleads us ;
We all believe we near the prize,
　Till some fresh dupe succeeds us !
And yet, tho' Life's a riddle, though
　No clerk has yet explain'd it,
I still can hope ; for well I know
　That Love has thus ordain'd it.

Paris, *November*, 1864.

ADVICE TO A POET.

Now if you'll only take, perchance
But half the pains to learn, that we
Still take to hide our ignorance—
How very clever you will be !

DEAR Poet, do not rhyme at all !
  But if you must, don't tell your neigh-
    bours,
Or five in six, who cannot scrawl,
  Will dub you donkey for your labours.
This epithet may seem unjust
  To you, or any verse-begetter :
Must we admit—I fear we must—
  That nine in ten deserve no better ?

Then let them bray with leathern lungs,
  And match you with the beast that
    grazes
Or wag their heads, and hold their
    tongues,
  Or damn you with the faintest praises.

Be patient, but be sure you won't
   Win vogue without extreme vexation :
Yet hope for sympathy,—but don't
   Expect it from a near relation.

When   strangers   first   approved   my
      books,
   My kindred marvell'd what the praise
      meant ;
Now they wear more respectful looks,
   But can't get over their amazement.
Indeed, they've power to wound, beyond
   That wielded by the fiercest hater,
For all the time they are so fond—
   Which makes the aggravation greater.
      *   *   *   *
Most warblers only half express
   The threadbare thoughts they feebly
      utter :
Now if they tried for something less,
   They might not sink, and gasp, and
      flutter.
Fly low at first,—then mount, and win
   The niche for which the town's con-
      testing ;

And never mind your kith and kin—
  But never give them cause for jesting.

Hold Pegasus in hand, control
  A taste for ornament ensnaring ;
Simplicity is yet the soul
  Of all that time deems worth the
    sparing.
Long lays are not a lively sport,
  So clip your own to half a quarter.
If readers now don't think them short,
  Posterity will cut them shorter.
    *   *   *   *

I look on bards who whine for praise
  With feelings of profoundest pity :
They hunger for the Poet's bays,
  And swear one's waspish when one's
    witty.
The critic's lot is passing hard—
  Between ourselves, I think reviewers,
When call'd to truss a crowing bard,
  Should not be sparing of the skewers.
    *   *   *   *

We all, the foolish and the wise,
  Regard our verse with fascination,

Through asinine-paternal eyes,
  And hues of fancy's own creation ;
Prythee, then, check that passing sneer
  At any self-deluded rhymer
Who thinks his beer (the smallest beer !)
  Has all the gust of *alt hochheimer*.
      *   *   *   *

Oh, for the Poet-Voice that swells
  To lofty truths, or noble curses—
I only wear the cap and bells,
  And yet some tears are in my verses.
I softly trill my sparrow reed,
  Pleased if but one should like the
    twitter ;
Humbly I lay it down to heed
  A music or a minstrel fitter.

AN ASPIRATION.

Alas, how deplorably love has miscarried,—
The stripling is dead, and the virgin is married!

I ASK'D Miss Di, who loves her sheep,
To look at this Arcadian peep
    Of April leafage, pure and beamy:
A pair of girls in hoops and nets
Have found a pair of woolly pets,
    And all is young, and *nice*, and
    dreamy.

Miss Di has kindly eyes for all
That's pretty, quaint, and pastoral :
    Said she, " These ladies sentimental
Are lucky, in a world of shams,
To find a pair of luckless lambs
    So white, and so extremely gentle."

I heard her with surprise and doubt,
For though I don't much care about
    The world she spoke with such dis-
    dain of ;

And though the lamb I mostly see
Is overdone, it seem'd to me
    That these had little to complain
    of.

When Beings of the fairer sex
Arrange their white arms round our
    necks,
    We are, we ought to be enrap-
    tured—
Would that I were your lamb, Miss Di,
Or even yon poor butterfly,
    With some small hope of being
    captured.

A GARDEN IDYLL.

There are plenty of roses (the patriarch speaks)
But alas not for me, on your lips and your cheeks ;
Sweet Maiden, rose laden—enough and to spare—
Spare, O spare me the rose that you wear in your
    hair.

WE have loiter'd and laugh'd in the
    flowery croft,
  We have met under wintry skies ;
Her voice is the dearest voice, and soft
  Is the light in her wistful eyes ;
It is sweet in the silent woods, among
  Gay crowds, or in any place
To hear her voice, to gaze on her young
    Confiding face.

For ever may roses divinely blow,
  And wine-dark pansies charm
By the prim box path where I felt the
    glow
  Of her dimpled, trusting arm,

And the sweep of her silk as she turn'd
    and smiled
    A smile as fair as her pearls ;
The breeze was in love with the darling
    child,
      As it moved her curls.

She show'd me her ferns and woodbine
    sprays,
    Foxglove and jasmine stars,
A mist of blue in the beds, a blaze
    Of red in the celadon jars :
And velvety bees in convolvulus bells,
    And roses of bountiful June—
Oh, who would think the summer spells
    Could die so soon !

For a glad song came from the milking
    shed,
    On a wind of that summer south,
And the green was golden above her
    head,
    And a sunbeam kiss'd her mouth ;
Sweet were the lips where that sunbeam
    dwelt—

And the wings of Time were fleet
As I gazed ; and neither spoke, for we
    felt
    Life was so sweet !

And the odorous limes were dim above
    As we leant on a drooping bough ;
And the darkling air was a breath of
    love,
    And a witching thrush sang " Now ! "
For the sun dropt low, and the twilight
    grew
    As we listen'd, and sigh'd, and leant—
That day was the sweetest day—and we
    knew
    What the sweetness meant.

1868.

ST. JAMES'S STREET.

(SEE NOTE.)

ST. JAMES'S STREET, of classic fame,
  The finest people throng it.
St. James's Street? I know the name,
  I think I've passed along it!
Why, that's where Sacharissa sigh'd
  When Waller read his ditty;
Where Byron lived, and Gibbon died,
  And Alvanley was witty.

A famous street! To yonder Park
  Young Churchill stole in class-time;
Come, gaze on fifty men of mark,
  And then recall the past time.
The *plats* at White's, the play at *Crock's*,
  The bumpers to Miss Gunning;
The *bonhomie* of Charlie Fox,
  And Selwyn's ghastly funning.

The dear old street of clubs and *cribs*,
   As north and south it stretches,
Still seems to smack of Rolliad squibs,
   And Gillray's fiercer sketches ;
The quaint old dress, the grand old
   style,
   The *mots*, the racy stories;
The wines, the dice, the wit, the bile—
   The hate of Whigs and Tories.

At dusk, when I am strolling there,
   Dim forms will rise around me ;—
Lepel flits past me in her chair,
   And Congreve's airs astound me !
And once Nell Gwynne, a frail young
   sprite,
   Look'd kindly when I met her;
I shook my head, perhaps,—but quite
   Forgot to quite forget her.

The street is still a lively tomb
   For rich, and gay, and clever ;—
The crops of dandies bud and bloom,
   And die as fast as ever.

Now gilded youth loves cutty pipes,
   And slang that's rather scaring,—
It can't approach its prototypes
   In taste, or tone, or bearing.

In Brummell's day of buckle shoes,
   Lawn cravats, and roll collars,
They'd fight, and woo, and bet—and lose
   Like gentlemen and scholars :
I'm glad young men should go the pace,
   I half forgive *Old Rapid ;*
These louts disgrace their name and
    race—
   So vicious and so vapid !

Worse times may come. *Bon ton,* in-
    deed,
   Will then be quite forgotten,
And all we much revere will speed
   From ripe to worse than rotten :
Let grass then sprout between yon
    stones,
   And owls then roost at Boodle's,
For Echo will hurl back the tones
   Of screaming *Yankee Doodles.*

I love the haunts of Old Cockaigne,
 Where wit and wealth were squan-
   der'd ;
The halls that tell of hoop and train,
 Where grace and rank have wander'd ;
Those halls where ladies fair and leal
 First ventured to adore me !—
Something of that old love I feel
 For this old street before me.

1867.

ROTTEN ROW.

Most people like to bill and coo,
  And some have done it for the last time ;
So, happy folk, we envy you
  Your pleasant and improving pastime.

I HOPE I'm fond of much that's good,
  As well as much that's gay ;
I'd like the country if I could ;
  I love the Park in May :
And when I ride in Rotten Row,
I wonder why they call'd it so.

A lively scene on turf and road ;
  The crowd is bravely drest :
The *Ladies' Mile* has overflow'd,
  The chairs are in request :
The nimble air, so soft, so clear,
Hardly can stir a ringlet here.

I'll halt beneath the pleasant trees,
  And drop my bridle-rein,

And, quite alone, indulge at ease
  The philosophic vein :
I'll moralise on all I see—
Yes, it was all arranged for me !

Forsooth, and on a livelier spot
  The sunbeam never shines.
Fair ladies here can talk and trot
  With statesmen and divines :
Could I have chosen, I'd have been
A Duke, a Beauty, or a Dean.

What grooms !   What gallant gentle-
      men !
  What well-appointed hacks !
What glory in their pace, and then
  What beauty on their backs !
My Pegasus would never flag
If weighted as my lady's nag.

But where is now the courtly troop
  That once rode laughing by ?
I miss the curls of Cantilupe,
  The laugh of Lady Di :
They all could laugh from night to morn,
And Time has laugh'd them all to scorn.

I then could frolic in the van
  With dukes and dandy earls ;
Then I was thought a *nice* young man
  By rather *nice* young girls !
I've half a mind to join Miss Browne,
And try one canter up and down.

Ah, no—I'll linger here a while,
  And dream of days of yore ;
For me bright eyes have lost the smile,
  The sunny smile they wore :—
Perhaps they say, what I'll allow,
That I'm not quite so handsome now.

1867.

A *NICE* CORRESPONDENT!

An angel at noon, she's a woman at night,
All softness, and sweetness, and love, and delight.

THE glow and the glory are plighted
    To darkness, for evening is come ;
The lamp in Glebe Cottage is lighted,
    The birds and the sheep-bells are
        dumb.
I'm alone for the others have flitted
    To dine with a neighbour at Kew :
I'm alone, but I'm not to be pitied—
    I'm thinking of you !

I wish you were here !   Were I duller
    Than dull, you'd be dearer than dear ;
I am drest in your favourite colour—
    Dear Fred, how I wish you were here !
I am wearing my lazuli necklace,
    The necklace you fasten'd askew !
Was there ever so rude or so reckless
    A darling as you ?

I want you to come and pass sentence
  On two or three books with a plot ;
Of course you know " Janet's Repent-
    ance " ?
  I'm reading Sir *Waverley* Scott,
The story of Edgar and Lucy,
  How thrilling, romantic, and true !
The Master (his bride *was* a goosey !)
    Reminds me of you.

They tell me Cockaigne has been
    crowning
  A Poet whose garland endures ;
It was you that first told me of Brown-
    ing,—
  That stupid old Browning of yours !
His vogue and his verve are alarming,
  I'm anxious to give him his due,
But, Fred, he's not nearly so charming
    A poet as you !

I heard how you shot at The Beeches,
  I saw how you rode *Chanticleer*,
I have read the report of your speeches,
  And echo'd the echoing cheer.

There's a whisper of hearts you are
    breaking,
Dear Fred, I believe it, I do !—
Small marvel that Folly is making
    Her idol of you !

Alas for the World, and its dearly
    Bought triumph, its fugitive bliss ;
Sometimes I half wish I were merely
    A plain or a penniless miss ;
But, perhaps, one is best with a "meas-
    ure
Of pelf," and I'm not sorry, too,
That I'm pretty, because 'tis a pleasure,
    My darling, to you !

Your whim is for frolic and fashion,
    Your taste is for letters and art ;—
This rhyme is the commonplace passion
    That glows in a fond woman's heart :
Lay it by in a dainty deposit
    For relics—we all have a few !
Love, some day they'll print it, because it
    Was written to you.

    1868.

AN OLD BUFFER.

BUFFER.—A cushion or apparatus, with strong springs, to deaden the buff or concussion between a moving body and one on which it strikes.—*Webster's English Dictionary.*

" *If Blossom's a sceptic, or saucy, I'll search,*
  And I'll find her a wholesome corrective—in Church! "

                          MAMMA *loquitur.*

"A KNOCK-ME-DOWN sermon, and worthy of Birch,"
Says I to my wife, as we toddle from church ;
" Convincing indeed ! " is the lady's re-mark ;
"How logical, too, on the size of the Ark ! "
Then Blossom cut in, without begging our pardons,
" Pa, was it as big as the 'Logical Gar-dens ? "

" Miss Blossom," says I to my dearest
    of dearies,
" Papa disapproves of nonsensical que-
    ries ;
The Ark was an Ark, and had people to
    build it,
Enough we are told Noah built it and
    fill'd it :
Mamma does not ask how he caught his
    opossums."
—Said she, " That remark is as foolish
    as Blossom's ! "

Thus talking and walking, the time is
    beguiled
By my orthodox wife and my sceptical
    child ;
I act as their *buffer*, whenever I can,
And you see I'm of use as a family
    man.
I parry their blows, I have plenty to
    do—
I think that the child's are the worst of
    the two !

My wife has a healthy aversion for
    sceptics,
She vows they are bad—they are only
    dyspeptics !
May Blossom prove neither the one nor
    the other,
But do as she's bid by her excellent
    mother.—
She thinks I'm a Solon ; perhaps, if I
    huff her,
She'll think I'm a—something that's
    denser and tougher.

TO LINA OSWALD.

(AGED FIVE YEARS.)

When vapid poets vex thee sore,
  Thy Mentor's old, and would remind thee,
That if thy griefs are all before,
  Thy pleasures are not all behind thee.

I TUMBLE out of bed betimes
To make my love these toddling rhymes;
And meet the hour, and meet the place
To bless her blythe good-morning face.
I send her all this heart can store;
I seem to see her as before,
An angel-child, divinely fair,
With meek blue eyes, and golden hair,
Curls tipt with changing light, that shed
A little glory round her head.

Has poet ever sung or seen a
Sweeter, wiser child than Lina?
Blue are her sash and snood, and blue's
The hue of her bewitching shoes;
But, saving these, she's virgin dight,
A happy creature clad in white.

Again she stands beneath the boughs,
Reproves the pup, and feeds the cows ;
Unvexed by rule, unscared by ill,
She wanders at her own sweet will ;
For what grave fiat could confine
My little charter'd libertine,
Yet free from feeling or from seeing
The burthen of her moral being ?

But change must come, and forms and
　　dyes
Will change before her changing eyes ;
She'll learn to blush, and hope, and
　　fear—
And where shall I be then, my dear ?

Little gossip, set apart
But one small corner of thy heart ;
Still there is one not quite employ'd,
So let me find and fill that void ;
Run then, and jump, and laugh, and
　　play,
But love me though I'm far away.

BROOMHALL, *September*, 1868.

ON "A PORTRAIT OF A LADY."

BY THE PAINTER.

I gathered it wet for my own sweet Pet
As we whisper'd and walk'd apart:
She gave me that rose, it is fragrant yet,—
And oh, it is near my heart.

SHE is good, for she must have a guile-
    less mind
With that noble, trusting air ;
A rose with a passionate heart is twined
    In her crown of golden hair.
Some envy the cross that caressingly
    dips
In her bosom, and some had died
For the promise of bliss on her red, red
    lips,
    And her thousand charms beside.

She is lovely and good ; she has peerless
    eyes ;—
    A haunting shape.   She stands

In a blossoming croft, under kindling
  skies ;
The weirdest of faery lands.
There are sapphire hills by the far-off
  seas,
  Grave laurels, and tender limes ;
They tremble and glow in the amorous
  breeze,
  —My Beauty is up betimes.

A bevy of idlers press around,
  To wonder, and wish, and loll ;
" Now who is the painter, and where
  has he found
The woman we all extol,
With her fresh young mouth, and her
  candid brow,
  And a bloom as of bygone days ? "
How natural sounds their worship, how
  Impertinent seems their praise !

I stand aloof ; I can well afford
  To pardon the babble and crush
As they praise a work (do I need re-
  ward ?)

That has grown beneath my brush :
Aloof—and, in fancy, again I hear
The music clash in the hall,
When they crown'd her Queen of their
dance and cheer,
—She is mine, and Queen of all !

Yes, my thoughts are away to that
happy day,
A few short months agone,
When we left the games, and the dance,
to stray
Through the dewy flowers, alone.
My feet are again among flowers divine,
Away from the noise and glare,
When I kiss'd her mouth, and her lips
press'd mine,—
And I fasten'd that rose in her hair.

1868.

THE MUSIC PALACE.

Shall you go?   I don't ask you to seek it or shun it ;
I went on an impulse, I've been and I've done it.

So this is a music-hall, easy and free,
A temple for singing, and dancing, and
    spree ;
The band is at *Faust*, and the benches
    are filling,
And all that I have can be had for a
    shilling.

The senses are charm'd by the sights
    and the sounds ;
A spirit of affable gladness abounds :
With zest we applaud, and as madly
    recall
The singer, the *cellar-flap-dancer*, and
    all.

What Vision comes on with a wreath
    and a lyre ?

A creature of impulse in scanty attire ;
She plays the good sprite in a dream-
  haunted dell,
She has ankles ! and eyes like a wistful
  gazelle.

A clown sings a song, and a droll cuts a
  caper,
And then she dissolves in a rose-colour'd
  vapour :
Then an imp on a rope is a painfully
  pleasant
Sensation for all the mammas that are
  present.

But who is the damsel that smiles to me
  there
With so reckless, indeed, so defiant an
  air ?
She is bright—that she's pretty is more
  than I'll say.
Is she happy ? At least she's exceedingly gay.

It seems to me now, as we pass up the
  street,

Is Nell worse than I, or the worthies we
  meet?
She is reckless, her conduct's exceedingly sad—
A coin may be light, but it need not be
  bad.

Heaven help thee, poor child: now a
  graceless and gay thing,
You once were your mother's, her pet
  and her plaything.
Where was your home? Are the stars
  that look down
On that home, the cold stars of this
  pitiless town?

The stars are a riddle we never may
  read—
I prest her poor hand, and I bade her
  Godspeed!
She left me a heart overladen with sor-
  row—
You may hear Nelly's laugh at the
  palace to-morrow!

Ah! some go to revel, and some go to
    rue,
For some go to ruin. There's Paul's
    tolling two.

A TERRIBLE INFANT.

I RECOLLECT a nurse call'd Ann,
   Who carried me about the grass,
And one fine day a fine young man
   Came up, and kiss'd the pretty lass:
She did not make the least objection !
               Thinks I, *"Aha !*
When I can talk I'll tell Mamma."
—And that's my earliest recollection.

WITH A BOOK OF SMALL
SKETCHES.

IN days gone by, and year by year,
I gleaned the sketchlets garnered here :
Some pains they cost me, much shoe
      leather
Before they all were got together.
Dear children, I must flit anon ;
O, guard them kindly when I'm gone.

AT HURLINGHAM.

THIS was dear Willy's brief despatch,
  A curt and yet a cordial summons;—
" Do come! I'm in to-morrow's match,
  And see us whip the *Faithful Com-
    mons.*"
We trundled out behind the bays,
  Through miles and miles of brick and
    garden ;
Mamma was drest in mauve and
    maize,—
  Of course I wore my *Dolly Varden.*

A charming scene, and lively too,
  The paddock's full, the band is play-
    ing
Boulotte's song in *Barbe bleue ;*
  And what are all these people saying?
They flirt! they bet! There's Linda
    Reeves

Too lovely !   I'd give worlds to borrow
Her yellow rose with russet leaves !—
   I'll wear a yellow rose to-morrow !

And there are May and Algy Meade ;
   How proud she looks on her promo-
      tion !
The ring must be amused indeed,
   And edified by such devotion !
I wonder if she ever guess'd !
   I wonder if he'll call on Friday !
I often wonder which is best !—
   I only hope my hair is tidy !

Some girls repine, and some rejoice,
   And some get bored, but I'm con-
      tented
To make my destiny my choice,—
   I'll never dream that I've repented.
There's something sad *in loved and
      cross'd*,
   For all the fond, fond hope that rings
      it :
There's something sweet in " loved and
      lost "—
   And Oh, how sweetly Alfred sings it !

I'll own I'm bored with *handicaps !*—
    Bluerocks ! (they always are " *blue-*
    rock"-ing !)—
With May, a little bit, perhaps,—
    And yon Faust's *teufelshund* is shock-
    ing !
Bang . . . bang . . . ! That's Willy !
    There's his bird,
    Blithely it cleaves the skies above
    me !
He's miss'd all ten ! He's too absurd !—
    I hope he'll always, always love me !

We've lost ! To tea, then back to
    town ;
    The crowd is laughing, eating, drink-
    ing :
The moon's eternal eyes look down,—
    Of what can yon sad moon be thinking
Oh, but for some good fairy's wand,—
    This pigeoncide is worse than silly,
But still I'm very, very fond
    Of Hurlingham, and tea,—and Willy.

UNREFLECTING CHILDHOOD.

The world would lose its finest joys
Without its little girls and boys ;
Their careless glee, and simple ruth,
And trust, and innocence, and truth.
—Ah, what would your poor poet do
Without such little folk as you ?

IT is, indeed, a little while
  Since you were born, my happy pet ;
Your future beckons with a smile,
  Your bygones don't exist as yet.
Is all the world with beauty rife ?
  Are you a little bird that sings
Her simple gratitude for life,
  And lovely things ?

The ocean, and the waning moons,
  And starry skies, and starry dells,
And winter sport, and golden Junes,
  Art, and divinest Beauty-spells :

Festa and song, and frolic wit,
   And banter, and domestic mirth,—
They all are ours !—dear child, is it
   A pleasant earth ?

And poet friends, and poesy,
   And precious books, for any mood :
And then that best of company,
   Those graver thoughts in solitude
That hold us fast and never pall :
   Then there is You, my own, my fair—
And I . . . soon I must leave it all,
   —And much you care.

1871.

LITTLE DINKY.

(A RHYME OF LESS THAN ONE.)

THE hair she means to have is gold,
Her eyes are blue, she's twelve weeks
    old,
    Plump are her fists and pinky.
She fluttered down in lucky hour
From some blue deep in yon sky bower—
    I call her LITTLE DINKY.

A Tiny now, ere long she'll please
To totter at my parent-knees,
    And crow, and try to chatter :
And soon she'll take to fair white frocks,
And frisk about in shoes and socks,—
    Her totter changed to patter.

And soon she'll play, ay, soon enough,
At cowslip-ball and blindman's-buff ;

And, some day, we shall find her
Grow weary of her toys—indeed
She'll fling them all aside to heed
    A footstep close behind her.

And years to come she'll still be rich
In what is left, the joys with which
    Our love can aye supply us ;
For hand in hand we'll sit us down
Right cheerfully and let the town—
    This foolish town, go by us.

Dinky, we must resign our toys
To younger girls, to finer boys,—
    But we'll not care a feather :
For then (reflection's not regret)
Tho' you'll be rather old ! we'll yet
    Be boy and girl together.

As I was climbing Ludgate Hill
I met a goose who dropt a quill,—
    You see my thumb is inky ;—
I fell to scribble there and then,
And this is how I came to pen
    These rhymes on LITTLE DINKY.

GERTRUDE'S NECKLACE.

As Gerty skipt from babe to girl,
Her necklace lengthen'd, pearl by pearl ;
Year after year it grew, and grew,
For every birthday gave her two.
Her neck is lovely, soft and fair,
And now her necklace glimmers there.

So cradled, let it sink and rise,
And all her graces emblemize.
Perchance this pearl, without a speck,
Once was as warm on Sappho's neck ;—
Where are the happy, twilight pearls
That braided Beatricé's curls ?

Is Gerty loved ?—Is Gerty loth ?
Or, if she's either, is she both ?
She's fancy free, but sweeter far
Than many plighted maidens are :
Will Gerty smile us all away,
And still be Gerty ?   Who can say ?

But let her wear her precious toy,
And I'll rejoice to see her joy :
Her bauble's only one degree
Less frail, less fugitive than we ;
For time, ere long, will snap the skein,
And scatter all the pearls again.

GERTRUDE'S GLOVE.

Elle avait au bout de ses manches
Une paire de mains si blanches !

SLIPS of a kid-skin deftly sewn,
A scent as through her garden blown,
The tender hue that clothes her dove,
All these, and this is Gerty's glove.

A glove but lately dofft, for look—
It keeps the happy shape it took
Warm from her touch !   What gave the
        glow ?
And where's the mould that shaped it so ?

It clasp'd the hand, so pure, so sleek,
Where Gerty rests a pensive cheek,
The hand that when the light wind stirs,
Reproves those laughing locks of hers.

You fingers four, you little thumb !
Were I but you, in days to come
I'd clasp, and kiss,—I'd keep her—go !
And tell her that I told you so.

KISSINGEN, *September*, 1871.

MABEL.

I.

AT HER WINDOW.

Ah, minstrel, how strange is
The carol you sing!
Let Psyche, who ranges
The garden of spring,
Remember the changes
December will bring.

BEATING heart! we come again
  Where my Love reposes :
This is Mabel's window-pane ;
  These are Mabel's roses.

Is she nested ?   Does she kneel
  In the twilight stilly ;
Lily clad from throat to heel,
  She, my virgin lily ?

Soon the wan, the wistful stars,
  Fading, will forsake her ;

Elves of light, on beamy bars,
  Whisper then, and wake her.

Let this friendly pebble plead
  At her flowery grating.
If she hear me will she heed ?
  Mabel, I am waiting.

Mabel will be deck'd anon,
  Zoned in bride's apparel ;
Happy zone !—Oh hark to yon
  Passion-shaken carol !

Sing thy song, thou trancèd thrush,
  Pipe thy best, thy clearest ;—
Hush, her lattice moves, O hush—
  Dearest Mabel !—dearest . . .

II.

HER MUFF.

LIVELY SHEPHERDESS.
Now mind,
He'll call on you to-morrow at eleven,
And beg that you will dine with us at seven ;
If, when He calls, you see that He has got
His green umbrella, then you'll know He'll not
Be going to the House, *and you'll decline,*
But if He hasn't it, you'll come and dine.

HAPPY SHEPHERD.

But if it rains: then how? and where? and when?
And how about the green umbrella then?

LIVELY SHEPHERDESS.

Then He'll be wet, that's all, for if I don't
Choose He should take it, why, of course! you goose!
He won't.

ARCADY.

SHE'S jealous! Does it grieve me? No!
I'm glad to see my Mabel so,
 Carina mia !
Poor Puss! That now and then she
  draws
Conclusions, not without a cause,
 Is my idea.

She loves ; and I'm prepared to prove
That jealousy is kin to love
 In constant women.
My jealous Pussy cut up rough
The day before I bought her muff
 With sable trimming.

These tearful darlings think to quell us
By being so divinely jealous ;
 But I know better.

Hillo ! Who's that ? A damsel ! Come,
I'll follow :—no, I can't, for some
　　One else has met her.

What fun !　He looks " a lad of grace."
She holds her muff to hide her face ;
　　They kiss,—The Sly Puss !
Hillo !　Her　muff,—it's　trimm'd　with
　　sable ! . .
It's like the muff I gave to Mabel ! . . .
　　Goodl-o-r-d, SHE'S *MY* PUSS !

TO LINA OSWALD.

(WITH A BIRTHDAY LOCKET.)

" My darling wants to see you soon,"—
I bless the little maid, and thank her ;
To do her bidding, night and noon
I draw on Hope—Love's kindest banker !

YOUR Sun is in brightest apparel,
   Your birds and your blossoms are gay,
But where is my jubilant carol
   To welcome so joyous a day ?
I sang for you when you were smaller,
   As fair as a fawn, and as wild :
Now, Lina, you're ten and you're taller—
      You elderly child.

I knew you in shadowless hours,
   When thought never came with a
     smart ;
You then were the pet of your flowers,
   And joy was the child of your heart.
I ever shall love you, and dearly !—
   I think when you're even thirteen

You'll still have a heart, and not merely
    A flirting machine!

And when time shall have spoil'd you of
    passion,—
  Discrown'd what you now think sub-
    lime,
Oh, I swear that you'll still be the fashion,
  And laugh at the antics of time.
To love you will then be no duty;
  But happiness nothing can buy—
There's a bud in your garland, my
    beauty,
        That never can die.

A heart may be bruised and not bro-
    ken,—
  A soul may despair and still reck;—
I send you, dear child, a poor token
  Of love, for your dear little neck.
The heart that will beat just below it
  Is open and pure as your brow—
May that heart, when you come to be-
    stow it,
        Be happy as now.

1869–1872.

THE REASON WHY.

Ask why I love the roses fair,
And whence they come and whose they
  were ;
They come from her, and not alone,
They bring her sweetness with their
  own.

Or ask me why I love her so,
I know not, this is all I know,
These roses bud and bloom, and twine
As she round this fond heart of mine.

And this is why I love the flowers,
Once they were hers, they're mine—
  they're ours !
I love her, and they soon will die,
And now you know the reason why.

A WINTER FANTASY.

December has brought you a bonnie May,—
A bonnie sweetheart is bound your way :
He is coming—tho' you little wot,—
You are waiting—yet he knows it not !

YOUR veil is thick, and none would
    know
    The pretty face it quite obscures ;
But if you foot it through the snow,
    Distrust those little boots of yours.

The tell-tale snow, a sparkling mould,
    Says where they go and whence they
      came,
Lightly they touch its carpet cold,
    And where they touch they sign your
    name.

She pass'd beneath yon branches bare,
    How fair her face, and how content !
I only know her face was fair,—
    I only know she came and went.

Pipe, robins, pipe; though boughs be
    bleak,
Ye are her winter choristers;
Whose cheek will press that rose-cold
    cheek?
What lips those fresh young lips of
    hers?

THE UNREALIZED IDEAL.

My only love is always near,—
    In country or in town
I see her twinkling feet, I hear
    The whisper of her gown.

She foots it ever fair and young,
    Her locks are tied in haste,
And one is o'er her shoulder flung,
    And hangs below her waist.

She ran before me in the meads ;
    And down this world-worn track
She leads me on ; but while she leads
    She never gazes back.

And yet her voice is in my dreams,
    To witch me more and more ;
That wooing voice ! Ah me, it seems
    Less near me than of yore.

Lightly I sped when hope was high,
   And youth beguiled the chase,—
I follow, follow still ; but I
   Shall never see her face.

IT MIGHT HAVE BEEN.

A FRIENDLY bird with bosom red
　Is fluting near my garden seat ;
Your sky is fair above my head,
　And Tweed rejoices at my feet.

The squirrels gambol in the oak,
　All, all is glad, but you prefer
To linger on amid the smoke
　Of stony-hearted Westminster.

Again I read your letter through,—
　" How wonderful is fate's decree,
How sweet is all your life to you,
　And oh, how sad is mine to me."

I know your wail—who knows it not ?—
　HE gave,—HE taketh that HE gave.
Yours is the lot, the common lot,
　To go down weeping to the grave.

Sad journey to a dark abyss,
   Meet ending of your sorrow keen,—
The burden of My dirge is this,
   And this My woe,—*It might have
     been!*

Dear bird! Blithe bird that sings in
    frost
   Forgive my friend if he is sad;
He mourns what he has only lost,—
   I weep what I have never had.

LEES, *September* 27, 1873.

LOVE, TIME, AND DEATH.

AH me, dread friends of mine—Love,
    Time, and Death !
  Sweet Love who came to me on sheeny
    wing,
And gave her to my arms—her lips, her
    breath,
  And all her golden ringlets clustering :
And Time who gathers in the flying
    years
He gave me all, but where is all he
    gave ?
He took my Love and left me barren
    tears,—
  Weary and lone I follow to the grave.
There Death will end this vision half
    divine,—
  Wan Death, who waits in shadow
    evermore,
And silent, ere he give the sudden sign ;

O, gently lead me thro' thy narrow
  door,
Thou gentle Death, thou trustiest friend
  of mine,
—Ah me for Love . . . *will* Death
  my Love restore?

THE OLD STONEMASON.

A SHOWERY day in early spring—
  An old man and a child
Are seated near a scaffolding
  Where marble blocks are piled.

His clothes are stain'd by age and soil,
  As hers by rain and sun ;
He looks as if his days of toil
  Were very nearly done.

To eat his dinner he had sought
  A staircase proud and vast,
And here the duteous child had brought
  His scanty noon repast.

A worn-out workman needing aid ;—
  A blooming child of light ;—
The stately palace steps ;—all made
  A most pathetic sight.

We had sought shelter from the storm,
  And saw this lowly pair,
But none could see a Shining Form
  That watch'd beside them there.

1874.

A RHYME OF ONE.

Explain why childhood's path is sown
With moral and scholastic tin tacks;
Ere sin (Original) was known,
Did Adam groan beneath the syntax?

YOU sleep upon your mother's breast,
    Your race begun,
A welcome, long a wish'd-for guest,
    Whose age is One.

A baby-boy, you wonder why
    You cannot run ;
You try to talk—how hard you try !—
    You're only One.

Ere long you won't be such a dunce ;
    You'll eat your bun,
And fly your kite, like folk, who once
    Were only One.

You'll rhyme, and woo, and fight, and
    joke,

Perhaps you'll pun !
Such feats are never done by folk
　　Before they're One.

Some day, too, you may have your joy,
　　And envy none ;
Yes, you, yourself, may own a boy,
　　Who isn't One.

He'll dance, and laugh, and crow, he'll
　　do
　　　As you have done :
(You crown a happy home, tho' you
　　Are only One).

But when he's grown shall you be here
　　To share his fun,
And talk of times when he (the dear !)
　　Was hardly One?

Dear child, 'tis your poor lot to be
　　My little son ;
I'm glad, though I am old, you see,—
　　While you are One.

1876.

MY SONG.

You ask a song,
Such as of yore, an autumn's even-
    tide,
Some blest boy-poet caroll'd,—and then
    died.
    Nay, *I* have sung too long.

    Say, shall I fling
A sigh to Beauty at her window-pane?
I sang there once, might I not once
    again?—
    Or tell me whom to sing.

    The peer of Peers?
Lord of the wealth that gives his time
    employ—
Time to possess, but hardly to enjoy—
    He cannot need *my* tears.

The man of *mind*,
Or priest, who darkens what is clear as
    day ?
I cannot sing them, yet I will not say
    Such guides are wholly blind.

    The Orator ?
He quiet lies where yon fresh hillock
    heaves :
'Twere well to sprinkle there those
    laurel-leaves
He won,—but never wore.

    Or shall I twine
The Cypress?　Wreath of glory and of
    gloom,—
To march a gallant soldier to his doom,
    Needs fuller voice than mine.

    No lay have I,
No murmured measure meet for your
    delight,
No song of Love and Death, to make
    you quite
    Forget that we must die.

Something is wrong,—
The world is over-wise ; or, more's the
pity,
These days are far too busy for a ditty,
Yet take it,—take my Song.

1876.

INCHBAE.

ANON he shuts the solemn book
To heed the falling of the brook,
He cares but little why it flows,
Or whence it comes, or where it goes.

For here, on this delightful bank,
His past—his future are a blank ;
Enough for him the bloom, the cheer,
They all are his, to-day and here.

But hark a voice that carols free,
And fills the air with melody !
She comes ! a creature clad in grace,
And gospel promise in her face.

So let her fearlessly intrude
On this his much loved solitude ;
Is she a lovely phantom, or
That love he long has waited for ?

* * * *

O welcome as the morning dew;
Long, long have I expected you;
Come, share my seat, and, late or soon,
All else that's mine beneath the moon.

And sing your happy roundelay
While nature listens.   Till to-day
This mirthful stream has never known
A cadence gladder than its own :

Forgive if I too fondly gaze,
Or praise the eyes that others praise :
I watch'd my Star, I've wander'd far—
Are you my joy?   You know you are!

Let others praise, as others prize,
The witching twilight of your eyes—
I cannot praise you : I adore,
And that is praise—and something more.

ANY POET TO HIS LOVE.

A rather sad man, still at times he was jolly,
And though hating a fool he'd a weakness for folly.

IMMORTAL VERSE! Is mine the strain
To last and live ? As ages wane
Will one be found to twine the bays,
And praise me then as now you praise ?

Will there be one to praise ? Ah no !
My laurel leaf may never grow ;
My bust is in the quarry yet,—
Oblivion weaves my coronet.

Immortal for a month—a week !
The garlands wither as I speak ;
The song will die, the harp's unstrung,—
But, singing, have I vainly sung ?

You deign'd to lend an ear the while
I trill'd my lay. I won your smile.

Now, let it die, or let it live,—
My verse was all I had to give.

The linnet flies on wistful wings,
And finds a bower, and lights and
            sings ;
Enough if my poor verse endures
To light, and live—to die in yours.

1875.

THE CUCKOO.

WE heard it calling, clear and low,
  That tender April morn ; we stood
  And listened in the quiet wood
We heard it, ay, long years ago.

It came, and with a strange, sweet cry,
  A Friend, but from a far-off land ;
  We stood and listened, hand in hand,
And heart to heart, my Love and I.

In dreamland then we found our joy,
  And so it seem'd as 'twere the Bird
  That Helen in old times had heard
At noon beneath the oaks of Troy.

O time far off, and yet so near !
  It came to her in that hush'd grove,
  It warbled while the wooing throve,
It sang the song she liked to hear.

And now I hear its voice again,
  And still its message is of peace,
  It sings of love that will not cease—
For me it never sings in vain.

HEINE TO HIS MISTRESS.

WHAT do the violets ail,
  So wan, so shy?
Why are the roses pale?
  Oh why? Oh why?

The lark sad music makes
  To sullen skies;
From yonder flowery brakes
  Dead odours rise.

Why is the sun's new birth
  A dawn of gloom?
Oh why is this fair earth
  My joyless tomb?

I wait apart and sigh
  I call to thee;
Why, Heart's-belovèd, why
  Didst thou leave me?

1876.

FROM THE CRADLE.

THEY tell me I was born a long
    Three months ago,
But whether they be right or wrong
    I hardly know.
I sleep, I smile, I cannot crawl,
    But I can cry :
At present I am rather small—
    A Babe am I.

The changing lights of sun and shade
    Are baby toys;
The flowers and birds are not afraid
    Of baby boys.
Some day I'll wish that I could be
    A bird and fly ;
At present I can't wish—you see
    A Babe am I.

THE TWINS.

YES, there they lie, so small, so quaint,
   Two mouths, two noses, and two chins;
What Painter shall we get to paint
   And glorify the Twins?
To give us all the charm that dwells
In tiny cloaks and coral-bells,
And all those other pleasant spells
Of Babyhood, and not forget
The silver mug for either Pet—
   No babe should be without it?
Come, Fairy Limner! you can thrill
Our hearts with pink and daffodil,
And white rosette, and dimpled frill;
Come, paint our little Jack and Jill,
   And don't be long about it!

AN EPITAPH.

HER worth, her wit, her loving smile
Were with me but a little while ;
She came, she went; yet though that
     Voice
Is hush'd that made the heart rejoice,
And though the grave is dark and chill,
Her memory is fragrant still,—
She stands on the eternal hill.

Here pause, kind soul, whoe'er you be,
And weep for her, and pray for me.

BABY MINE.

BABY mine, with the grave, grave face,
  Where did you get that royal calm,
Too staid for joy, too still for grace?
  I bend as I kiss your pink, soft palm;
Are you the first of a nobler race,
                    Baby mine?

You come from the region of *long ago*,
  And gazing awhile where the seraphs
    dwell
Has given your face a glory and glow—
  Of that brighter land have you ought
    to tell?
I seem to have known it—I more would
    know,
                    Baby mine.

Your calm, blue eyes have a far-off
    reach,
  Look at me now with those wondrous
    eyes,
Why are we doom'd to the gift of
    speech
  While you are silent, and sweet, and
    wise ?
You have much to learn—you have more
    to teach,
              Baby mine.

DU RYS DE MADAME D'ALLE-BRET.

HOW fair those locks which now the light
    wind stirs !
  What eyes she has, and what a per-
    fect arm !
And yet methinks that little Laugh of
    hers—
  That little Laugh is still her crowning
    charm.
Where'er she passes, country-side or
    town,
  The streets make festa, and the fields
    rejoice.
Should sorrow come, as 'twill, to cast
    me down,
  Or Death, as come he must, to hush
    my voice,
Her Laugh would wake me, just as now
    it thrills me—
  That little giddy Laugh wherewith she
    kills me.

THE LADY I LOVE.

THE Lady I sing is as charming as
    Spring,
I own that I love the dear Lady I sing :
She is gay, she is sad, she is good, she
    is fair,
She lives at a Number in —— —— —— Square.

It is not 21, it is not 23—
You never shall get her Number from
    me ;
If you did, very soon you'd be mounting
    the stair
Of Number (no matter what!) —— —— ——
    Square.

They say she is clever. Indeed it is
    said
She is making a Novel right out of her
    Head !

That poor little Head! If her heart were
    to spare,
I'd break, and I'd mend it in — — —
    Square.

I've a heart of my own, and, in prose as
    in rhymes,
This heart has been fractured a good
    many times ;
An excellent heart, tho' in sorry repair—
Little Friend, may I mend it in — — —
    Square ?

"*What nonsense you talk.*" Yes, but
    still I am one
Who feels pretty grave when he seems
    full of fun ;
Some people are pretty, and yet full of
    care—
And Some One is pretty in — — —
    Square.

I know I am singing in old-fashion'd
    phrase
The music that pleased in the old-
    fashion'd days ;

Alas, I know, too, I've an old-fashion'd
    air—
Oh, why did I ever see — — — Square!

POSTSCRIPT.

The writer of prose, by intelligence taught,
Says the thing that will please, in the way that
    he ought,
But your poor despised Bard, who by Nature
    is blest,
(In the scope of a couplet, or guise of a jest,)
Says the thing that he pleases as pleases him
    best.

OUR PHOTOGRAPHS.

She play'd me false, but that's not why
I haven't quite forgiven Di,
      Although I've tried :
This curl was hers, so brown, so bright,
She gave it me one blissful night,
      And—more beside !

Our photographs were group'd together ;
She wore the darling hat and feather
      That I adore ;
In profile by her side I sat
Reading my poetry—but that
      She'd heard before.

Why, after all, Di threw me over
I never knew, I can't discover,
      And hardly guess ;
May be Smith's lyrics she decided
Were sweeter than the sweetest I did—
      I acquiesce.

A week before their wedding day,
That Beast was call'd in haste away
    To join the Staff.
Di gave him then, with tearful mien,
Her only photograph.   I've seen
    That photograph,

I've seen it in Smith's pocket-book!
Just think! her hat, her tender look,
    Are now that Brute's !
Before she gave it, off she cut
My body, head and lyrics, but
She was obliged, the little Slut,
    To leave my Boots.

MA FUTURE.

WE parted, but again I stopt
  To greet her at the door,
Her thimble, mine the gift, had dropt
  Unheeded to the floor.

Her eyes met mine, her eyelids fell
  To veil their sweet content ;
Her happy blush and kind *farewell*
  Were with me as I went.

And when I join'd the human tide
  And turmoil of the street,
A Spirit-form was at my side,
  And gladness wing'd my feet.

Exultingly the world went by,
  The town and I were gay !
And one far stretch of soft blue sky
  Seem'd leading me away.

I left her happy, and I know
  That we shall meet anon ;
I left my Love an hour ago,
  And yet she is not gone.

MY NEIGHBOUR'S WIFE!

HARK ! hark to my neighbour's flute !
Yon powder'd slave, that ox, that ass
    are his :
Hark to his wheezy pipe ; my neigh-
    bour is
    A worthy sort of brute.

    My tuneful neighbour's rich — has
    houses, lands,
A wife (confound his flute)—a handsome
    wife !
Her love must give a gusto to his life.
    See yonder—there she stands.

    She turns, she gazes, she has lustrous
    eyes,
A throat like Juno and Aurora's arms—
Per Bacco, what a paragon of charms !
    My neighbour's drawn a prize.

Yet, somehow, life's a nuisance with
    its woes,
Disease and doubt—and that eternal
    preaching :
We've suffer'd from our early pious
    teaching—
    We suffer—goodness knows.

How vain the wealth that breeds its
    own vexation !
Yet few of us would care to quite fore-
    go it :
Then weariness of life—and many know
    it—
    Is not a glad sensation :

And therefore, neighbour mine, with-
    out a sting
I contemplate thy fields, thy house, thy
    flocks,
I covet not thy man, thine ass, thine ox,
    Thy flute, thy—anything.

ARCADY.

LIVELY SHEPHERDESS.

Now mind,
He'll call on you to morrow at eleven,
And beg that you will dine with us at
    seven ;
If, when He calls, you see that He has
    got
His green umbrella, then you'll know
    He'll not
Be going to the House, and you'll decline,
But if He hasn't it, you'll come and dine.

HAPPY SHEPHERD.

But if it rains : then how? and where ?
    and when ?
And how about the green umbrella then ?

LIVELY SHEPHERDESS.

Then He'll be Wet, that's all, for if I
    don't
Choose He should take it, why, of course!
    you goose ! he won't.

A KIND PROVIDENCE.

HE dropt a tear on Susan's bier,
   He seem'd a most despairing Swain ;
But bluer sky brought newer tie,
   And—would he wish her back again ?
The moments fly, and when we die,
   Will Philly Thistletop complain ?
She'll cry and sigh, and—dry her eye,
   And let herself be woo'd again.

NOTES.

NOTES.

" St. George's, Hanover Square."

" Dans le bonheur de nos meilleurs amis nous trouvons souvent quelque chose qui ne nous plaît pas entièrement."

"A Human Skull."

" In our last month's Magazine you may remember there were some verses about a portion of a skeleton. Did you remark how the poet and present proprietor of the human skull at once settled the sex of it, and determined off-hand that it must have belonged to a woman ? Such skulls are locked up in many gentlemen's hearts and memories. Blue-beard, you know, had a whole museum of them —as that imprudent little last wife of his found out to her cost. And, on the other hand, a lady, we suppose, would select hers of the sort which had carried beards when in the flesh."—*Adventures of Philip on his Way* *through the World. Cornhill Magazine, January,* 1861.*

"TO MY OLD FRIEND POSTUMUS."

The Well-beloved!—B. L. died 26th July, 1853.

"TO MY MISTRESS."

M. Deschanel quotes the following charming little poem by Corneille, addressed to a young lady who had not been quite civil to him. He says with truth—" Le sujet est léger, le rhythme court, mais on y retrouve la fierté de l'homme, et aussi l'ampleur du tragique." The last four stanzas, in particular, are brimful of spirit, and the mixture of pride and vanity they display is remarkable.

"Marquise, si mon visage
A quelques traits un peu vieux,
Souvenez-vous, qu'à mon âge
Vous ne vaudrez guère mieux.

---

* When I first sent these lines to the Cornhill Magazine, Mr. Thackeray, the editor, and an admirable judge of verse, proposed an alteration in the third stanza, and he returned it to me as it now stands. Originally I had made it to run thus :—

Did she live yesterday, or ages sped?
What colour were the eyes when bright and waking?
And were your ringlets fair? Poor little head!
. —Poor little heart! that long has done with aching

" Le temps aux plus belles choses
　Se plaît à faire un affront,
　Et saura faner vos roses
　Comme il a ridé mon front.

" Le même cours des planètes
　Règle nos jours et nos nuits ;
　On m'a vu ce que vous êtes,
　Vous serez ce que je suis.

" Cependant j'ai quelques charmes
　Qui sont assez éclatants
　Pour n'avoir pas trop d'alarmes
　De ces ravages du temps.

" Vous en avez qu'on adore,
　Mais ceux que vous méprisez
　Pourraient bien durer encore
　Quand ceux-là seront usés.

" Ils pourront sauver la gloire
　Des yeux qui me semblent doux,
　Et dans mille ans faire croire
　Ce qu'il me plaira de vous.

" Chez cette race nouvelle
　Où j'aurai quelque crédit,
　Vous ne passerez pour belle
　Qu'autant que je l'aurai dit.

" Pensez-y, belle Marquise,
　Quoiqu'un grison fasse effroi,
　Il vaut qu'on le courtise
　Quand il est fait comme moi."

"THE ROSE AND THE RING."

MR. THACKERAY spent a portion of the winter of 1854 in Rome, and while there he wrote his little Christmas story called "The Rose and the Ring." He was a great friend of the distinguished American sculptor, Mr. Story, and was a frequent visitor at his house. I have heard Mr. Story speak with emotion of the kindness of Mr. Thackery to his little daughter, then recovering from a severe illness, and he told me that Mr. Thackeray used to come nearly every day to read to Miss Story, often bringing portions of his manuscript with him.

Five or six years afterwards Miss Story showed me a very pretty copy of "The Rose and the Ring," which Mr. Thackeray had sent her, with a facetious sketch of himself in the act of presenting her with the work.

"NUPTIAL VERSES."

THESE lines were published in 1863 in "A Welcome," dedicated to the Princess of Wales; and "An Aspiration" was written for two Woodcuts in "A Round of Days." (Christmas, 1865.)

"THE JESTER'S MORAL."

" I WISH that I could run away
From House, and Court, and Levee :
Where bearded men appear to-day,
Just Eton boys grown heavy."

W. M. PRAED.

"A Garden Idyll."

WHEN these verses appeared in *Macmillan's Magazine* they ran as follows, but many of my readers could not see the point, and others, seeing it, disliked it so heartily, that I altered them in sheer vexation; now they have two readings, and can take their choice.

GERALDINE AND I.

Di te, Damasippe, deæque
Verum ob consilium donent tonsore.

I HAVE talk'd with her often in noon-day heat,
  We have walk'd under wintry skies ;
Her voice is the dearest voice, and sweet
  Is the light in her gentle eyes ;
It is bliss in the silent woods, among
  Gay crowds, or in any place,
To mould her mind, to gaze in her young
  Confiding face.

For ever may roses divinely blow,
  And wine-dark pansies charm
By that prim box path where I felt the glow
  Of her dimpled, trusting arm,
And the sweep of her silk as she turn'd and
    smiled
  A smile as fair as her pearls ;
The breeze was in love with the darling child,
  And coax'd her curls.

She show'd me her ferns and woodbine sprays,
  Foxglove and jasmine stars,
A mist of blue in the beds, a blaze
  Of red in the celadon jars :
And velvety bees in convolvulus bells,
  And roses of bountiful Spring.
But I said—"Though roses and bees have
    spells,
    They have thorn and sting."

She show'd me ripe peaches behind a net
  As fine as her veil, and fat
Gold fish a-gape, who lazily met
  For her crumbs—I grudged them that !
A squirrel, some rabbits with long lop ears,
  And guinea-pigs, tortoise-shell—wee ;
And I told her that eloquent truth inheres
    In all we see.

I lifted her doe by its lops, quoth I,
  " Even here deep meaning lies,—
Why have squirrels these ample tails, and why
  Have rabbits these prominent eyes ? "
She smiled and said, as she twirl'd her veil,
  " For some nice little cause, no doubt—
If you lift a guinea-pig up by the tail
    His eyes drop out ! "
  1868.

" ST. JAMES'S STREET."

I HOPE my readers, whoever they may be, will
not credit me with all the sentiments expressed
in this volume. I am told that these lines

have disturbed some Americans, but surely without cause. The remark in the seventh stanza is natural in the mouth of a rather exclusive habitué of St. James's, who has the mortification to feel that he is no longer young, who is too shallow-minded to appreciate our advance in civilisation during the last forty years, but who is nevertheless sufficiently keen to see what is possible in the future. My friends know I have a sincere admiration for the American people.

"A *NICE* CORRESPONDENT."

ERE long, perhaps in the next generation, the word NICE, and some other equally common words, may have passed into the limbo of *elegant*, *genteel*, &c. Fashions change, and certain words sink in the scale of gentility, and pass, like houses, into the hands of humbler occupants. But what can poor poets do !

"A WINTER FANTASY."

THE two first stanzas are imitated from Théophile Gautier.

THE kind of verse I have attempted in *some* of the pieces in this volume was in repute during the era of Swift and Prior, and again during the earlier years of this century. Af-

terwards it fell into comparative neglect, but
has now regained a little of its old popularity.

Herrick, Suckling, Waller, Swift, Prior,
Cowper, Landor, Moore, Praed, and Thackeray may be considered its representative men,
and each has his peculiar merit. Herrick is a
finished artist, with a delightful feeling and
fancy, and some of his flower-pieces are as
perfect as anything of the kind in the language. We admire Suckling for his gusto,
and careless, natural grace ; while Waller has
never been equalled for the way in which he
blends his courtly wit and rhythmic elegance ;
his lines " To a Rose," and " On a Girdle," in
these respects, leave nothing to be desired.
Swift is pre-eminent for the intensity of his
mordant humour, as Prior for his genial and
sprightly wit, or as Hazlitt very happily ex-
presses it, his " *mischievous gaiety.*" Cowper
is a master of tender and playful irony. Landor is wanting in humour and variety, but he
atones for it by his pathos, and his pellucid
and classical style. Moore, as a satirist, is a
very expert swordsman, and although there is
rather too much tinsel in his sentiment, he has
wit, and fun, and music, and sparkling fancy
in abundance. Praed has considerable fancy,
but it is less wild than Moore's, while his sym-
pathies are narrower than Thackeray's ; he
has plenty of wit, however, and a highly idiomatic, incisive, and most finished style, and, in
his peculiar vein, has never been equalled.

and it may be safely affirmed, never can be ex-
celled. What am I to say of Thackeray? As
he is yet rather too near to us, I will not criti-
cize him; but I may observe that he is almost
as humorous as Swift, and occasionally almost
as tender as Cowper, and one does not exactly
see why he might not have been as good an artist as most of those above mentioned.

Lovelace has given us one or two little
poems, by no means perfect, but which in
their way are admirable. The gay and gallant
Colonel is at this moment one of our really
popular minor poets, and all for the sake of
some two short pages of verse! Marlowe,
Wotton, Ben Jonson, Raleigh, and Montrose
must not be forgotten, as all have written ex-
cellently; not to speak of Carew, Sedley, Par-
nell ("When thy beauty appears"), Pope,
Gray, Goldsmith, Captain Morris (" I'm often
asked by plodding Souls "), Canning (the immortal " Needy Knife-grinder "), Luttrell,
Rogers, Coleridge, Mrs. Barbauld (" Human
Life"), W. R. Spencer, the brothers Smith
(the inimitable " Rejected Addresses"),
Haynes Bayly, Dr. Barham, Peacock (" Love
and Age "), Francis Mahony (" The Bells of
Shandon"), Leigh Hunt, Hood, Lord Macau-
lay ("A Valentine "), Mrs. Browning, and
many others, dead and living.

Light lyrical verse should be short, elegant,
refined, and fanciful, not seldom distinguished
by chastened sentiment, and often playful, and

it should have one uniform and simple design. The tone should not be pitched high, and the language should be idiomatic, the rhythm crisp and sparkling, the rhyme frequent and never forced, while the entire poem should be marked by tasteful moderation, high finish, and completeness ; for however trivial the subject matter may be, indeed rather in proportion to its triviality, subordination to the rules of composition, and perfection of execution, should be strictly enforced. Each piece cannot be expected to exhibit all these characteristics, but the qualities of brevity and buoyancy are essential.

It should also have the air of being spontaneous ; indeed, to write it well is a difficult accomplishment, and no one has fully succeeded in it without possessing a certain gift of irony, which is not only a rarer quality than humour, or even wit, but is altogether less commonly met with than is sometimes imagined. The poem may be tinctured with a well-bred philosophy, it may be gay and gallant, it may be playfully malicious or tenderly ironical, it may display lively banter, and it may be satirically facetious, it may even, considering it as a mere work of art, be pagan in its philosophy or trifling in its tone, but it must never be ponderous or commonplace. It is needless to say that good sense will be found to underlie all the best poetry of whatever kind. There are good poets whose productions are more pol-

ished than finished, their stanzas are less per‚
fect than their single lines, and their whole
poems are not so satisfactory as either ; and
again there are better poets who are more finished than polished; now it seems to me that
both qualities are peculiar to, and are pretty
equally balanced in the best productions of the
authors I have mentioned above.

It is interesting to see what Voltaire* says
of rhyme, its value, and its difficulties, and
then to observe with how little success it is
usually practised. Rhyme and alliteration
cannot be too important features in burlesque
verse. They may be prominent in satire and
semi-humorous poetry, but their presence
should be less and less marked as the poem
rises in tone. It is consoling to find that the
most worn and the worst used rhymes and
metres instantly recover all their charm and
freshness in the hands of a master.

This volume is now arranged finally. It is
with diffidence that I again offer it to the pub-
lic. No one is so painfully aware as myself of
its many shortcomings, its extreme insignifi-

---

* " We insist that the rhyme shall cost nothing to the
ideas, that it shall neither be trivial, nor too far-fetched ;
we exact rigorously in a verse the same purity, the
same precision, as in prose. We do not admit the
smallest license ; we require an author to carry without
a break all these chains, and yet that he should appear
ever free."

cance, and its great incompleteness, and I
never felt it more keenly than now, in sending
out this the eighth edition.   My dear reader,
if I have included pieces which ought to have
been consigned to the dust-bin of immediate
oblivion, I hope you will forgive me.

THE END.